OPEN WATER

"Oh, papa,—papa—" she was saying, and believe me, I didn't
regret that finish

OPEN WATER

BY

JAMES BRENDAN CONNOLLY

AUTHOR OF "OUT OF GLOUCESTER," "THE SEINERS,"
"THE DEEP SEA'S TOLL," "THE CRESTED SEAS," ETC.

WITH ILLUSTRATIONS

CHARLES SCRIBNER'S SONS
NEW YORK::::::::::::::::::::::1910

CONTENTS

ILLUSTRATIONS

THE EMIGRANTS

THE EMIGRANTS

The Emigrants

TO the waiting people in Poland there came one day the most momentous package of all, that which contained the money for their tickets—this from far-away America, from Henry, good husband to Esther, and more than a son to Esther's mother, even from the day he had asked her for Esther in marriage.

Then were there the most formidable details to be attended to; for in the realm of the Czar the matter of emigrating is of great moment. There had to be faced the most terrifying of officials, who asked the most searching questions, and gave over the papers only after the most rigid formalities, and also only after payments had been made that seemed like mountains of expense to people who for so long had been dwelling in the valley of poverty.

And there was even more than that. When for so many hundreds of years one's ancestors have lived and died in a country—in so many cases for that country—one does not, generally, make ready to leave that country, forever most likely, and for a far-away and unknown land most surely, without making some little stir, without betraying to the neighbors something of the inward agitation; hardly even, though that country be one long ruled by people of a later creation and cruder civilization, by aliens who for some centuries now had been denying all ancestral rights.

But the day of departure came at last, and with the unnecessary household effects disposed of, the little patch of land handed over, the passports obtained—all that attended to—and the last-made grave visited once again, Esther and Esther's mother, with the four children, emerged from beneath the shower of tears, kisses, embraces, and blessings, and boarded the rough car on which they were to be jolted to the frontier.

The frontier! They were near to it at length, and nearing it were met by uniformed officials of the country they were leaving, who peered into their faces, shouted at them, examined their papers, went away, came back, had another look, another examination, shouted once more, and finally allowed the train to pass beyond the line of pacing soldiers, and thence to the servants of the great steamship companies, more especially the one in green livery with red trimmings, who also shouted at them—everybody seemed to shout at them, but this one could be heard a league—

The Emigrants

"D'Auswanderer—Auswanderer!" And when he made it clear that they were to rally to him, and they had humbly assembled, turned them over to a little old man, also in uniform, who re-assembled them after his own fashion, and led them like a band of conscripts to the company's lodging-house and there assigned them quarters for the night. The company, the little man made them understand, was now responsible for them—from now until they were aboard the steamer in Hamburg; and though the company would be a kind father to them, it would also see that none strayed beyond the confines of its premises.

They were happy then; and Esther's mother, who had not from the first moment of departure ceased to worry for the children, above all for little Michel, now in deep gratitude put them away for the night, the eldest two in one berth, the next with Esther. Michel, the youngest—the baby—she took to herself. Never would she part from little Michel—never—never—and told him so between the lines of the song with which she lulled him to sleep.

To the women, when the children were hushed, there came from the next apartment the sound of men's voices. One there was who seemed to have come back from America for a holiday—a young man, by the tone—recounting tales of the wonderful land to which all were bound. Not longer than two days was he in New York when some one said, "Come," and set him to work at two dollars—two dollars—four rubles, a day—yes.

In a berth opposite to Esther's mother, a young woman breathed aloud at that. "You heard, old mother? Four rubles a day. You have no man, but it is fine to think of, is it not?"

"Truly," answered Esther's mother, "it will be fine for the young."

Esther's mother could then hear old Joseph asking questions. Poor old Joseph! For him there had been no need to come. He had, indeed, saved enough to keep him, with prudence, all his years at home. But he had come, and there was no gainsaying him. To the frontier only—to the control station, no further—he had said to the neighbors, and even to themselves, before taking the train; but to America it was to be, in truth, as he had told them that afternoon in the cars, and told them also how he had sold his little possessions privately, and drawn all his savings, and changed all into large bills which, even at the moment, were in a pouch under his vest. He even showed them where, around his neck, under his long white beard, lay the string of the pouch.

They slept well that night. The cooing and gurgling of little Michel awoke Esther's mother,

as it had awakened her for many mornings now.
What a feeling that—the little fingers creeping
up over the face and trying to open one's eyes in
the morning! Oh, the little man! she cuddled
him and kept him by her until long after Esther
had the other children ready—until the company's man came to say that those who cared
might cook breakfast in the kitchen below where
were samovars and charcoal, and where cold water
was to be had of the pump in the yard outside.
After that they must be ready to go to the office,
there to get tickets, for which one must have the
money ready.

"Children under four years are free at the
steamship from Hamburg to New York, but only
those under ten months are free at the railway
from here to Hamburg. Be prepared!"

"Oh, my little Michel! We shall have to pay
for him on the railway, think you, Esther?—and
he but hardly weaned."

"And for Max on the steamer, mother. He is
five."

"Five—yes—but small for his age. Michel is
such a great fellow."

Just before Esther's mother in the line was the
young woman who had slept in the berth opposite Esther's mother during the night. She held
a lusty baby boy in her arms. The weight of

him was sagging one hip and shoulder down and around, but she would not set him down.

To her came the superintendent: a portly, good-looking man in a thin silk coat, fine, frilled linen, loose tie, and the softest of tanned kid slippers, and a clerk at his elbow with pad and pen.

"And this one—how old is he?"

The young woman trembled. Esther's mother, next in line, also trembled.

"How old, I say—how old?"

"Ten months, Your Excellence."

"Ten months? Ten months? Set him down."

"But he cannot walk yet—he is too young, Your Excellence."

"Pish—pish—for a moment, and let us see. There—and he cannot walk, you say?"

"Oh, but so little, Your Excellence." Fat, curly, bow-legged, and black-eyed, the child stamped about the room.

"But so little, you say, and only ten months? So. At ten years he will be a man already. Ten months! and walks like a sailor. Ten months!"

"He was born so, Your Excellence—large and strong for his age."

"So." The superintendent halted to wipe his perspiring cheeks. "Ah, but it is warm. And this other fat, curly one?" he pinched little Michel's cheek. "What age? Ten months, also, old mother?"

"Ten months, Your Excellence."

"And born large and strong also? And his name—Samson? No? Michel, you say? Oh, Michel! Ach! let them pass. Let them all pass. What can one do with women—such lies! To the doctor now."

To the first room in the control station went Esther's party, and these, with many others, patiently awaited examination.

Laws! There were laws, it seemed. And had they not left all troublesome laws behind them? And here, regulations also—such queer things were in the world! which said that they must be examined all, especially as to hair and eyes, before they would be allowed on the railway which was to take them, by and by, to the steamship and so on to the great country beyond the great sea.

It was terrifying, this waiting in line; and then, when the doctor said, "Now you—" to have to march up the whole length of the long room and stand before him, with his eyes and mouth that did not smile, and have him look one over so— such a look! and the looking-glass that was strapped to his forehead! It could not be that he knew how he frightened one when he studied one out in that way—so—and shook his hands slowly—so—and then stiff and stern—so! No, surely he could not know.

Behind Esther was the old mother, holding little Michel, dancing him up and down, sticking her face into his face, saying boo! and boo! and boo! again, and kissing him every time he crowed aloud. This was her own darling—youngest of all—little Michel. She held him high over her shoulder that he might stroke old Joseph's beard, and old Joseph, sad and patient, for a moment tried to smile.

Esther faced the doctor, and, being passed, came back to her place on the long bench. Esther's mother should have been next, but she turned to Joseph, and he, obedient as in the days of his youth, stood before the doctor. The doctor took up his paper.

"You are alone?"

"Yes, Herr Doctor."

"No wife, no child behind you?"

"No wife, nor child—nor kin, Herr Doctor."

"And in America—no kin?"

"Nobody—in all the world, nobody."

"But at your age—why do you go? You like to travel?"

"I? Not I—old trees, fast roots."

"So? But tell me—it is for myself, not the law, that I ask—why do you go?"

The Emigrants

"I go because my friends go. Esther goes—and so the children. The children go, so goes Sarah; and where Sarah goes even there must I go."

"So? And which is Sarah?"

"She who is next."

"With the child? H-m—she is old also."

"She has been younger, Herr Doctor."

"I meant no harm, old man. That you **may** know her when she is yet older is my wish."

"May the Lord spare her, Herr Doctor. And if I may say it—you will see for yourself—the child is her life."

"'Tis not hard to see that. But if you will step down now and tell her to come."

Sarah approached haltingly. She still carried Michel.

"That child—is he not heavy, old mother?"

"Oh, no, Herr Doctor—not little Michel!"

"But you must set him down now."

"And I must, Herr Doctor?"

"Only for a little while. That is it. And now the hair."

Down tumbled the hair. Old Joseph remembered what that hair was once, and, remembering, sighed.

"And now for the eyes. The head this way—so."

The Emigrants

The faded old eyes were turned toward the light. They looked like eyes that had wept so much they could weep no more.

"So—h-m— And now this way. And this way once more. H-m-m— You have seen much trouble, old mother?"

"Trouble? Every one has trouble."

"It is true. And your daughter—she is the only child now?"

"The only child."

"There were others?"

"Five are buried, Herr Doctor—five and their father."

"Ah! and your daughter's husband, is it not, who sends the money for passage?"

"Henry it is—yes. A fine boy, and who has worked so hard that we might all come to him together."

"So." Longer, and yet longer, the doctor looked into the old eyes. Then he asked her further questions. Afterward she could not remember what the questions were—he asked so many—and there was that fearful looking-glass on his head; but she told him of the sickness with her eyes. She had had that sickness with her eyes for a long time now. But it mattered little. She could see to sew in the long nights of winter and to make all the clothes for the babies. And no one had ever before said that her eyes were not as good for that as any other eyes. The very clothes that little Michel then had on—where was he, the little imp? Oh, under the table—such a boy! those clothes were the envy of every mother in the village. And her own eyes had overlooked every stitch, every single stitch. Look, the Herr Doctor could see for himself that the work was well done. Not another child in the village had such clothes. Children of the rich there were with clothes that would not show finer stitching.

The surgeon, shaking his head, turned to the superintendent. She could not understand what it was they said, the one to the other—they talked in Polish no longer—but there was that in their faces and gestures which troubled her. She put her hand on the surgeon's arm even before he had done speaking to the superintendent, and all in the room trembled for her boldness. Her other hand clasped little Michel's fingers.

Then the superintendent, who seemed to talk all languages—and her own language as one born to it—called Esther over and whispered to her. And Esther mournfully told her mother that she would have to wait for a time.

"Wait? And why?" It was plain she did not understand.

"There is not money enough for all, His Excellence says. It is full fare for children over four years of age, and half fare for children over ten months. And Max is above four years, and little Michel above ten months—they have decided. And if the children are to go, some one must stay behind—is it not so, Your Excellence?"

"It is so, old mother," confirmed the superintendent.

Esther's mother looked to her little Michel, and from him around the room. Her eyes fastened on the slim young woman with the fat baby in arms, she who had been in the opposite berth the night before, and just ahead of them in line at the office. All had remarked that since leaving the office that morning not once had she set her baby down. She feared to have to buy a ticket for him—'twas not hard to see that. To her Esther's mother rushed. "See, Herr Excellence, see you, which is the larger? Or, the Herr Doctor, who understands such things better, see, which is the older—this one or my little Michel. Set him down—will you not set him down? Ah, she will not. Look again, Herr Doctor. This one has been passed, has he not?"

"It is true," said the superintendent.

Then did Esther's mother force the young woman to set the fat baby on the floor. In an instant he was rolling toward the men.

The Emigrants

"Ten months, and see him run! Ten months, and free! But not little Michel?" With her dry eyes she faced the superintendent. "But not little Michel, Herr Doctor?"

The surgeon shook his head. The soul was not open to his knife. Then, suddenly, he wondered why he was spending so much time over this case. Again and again had such cases come before him —not exactly alike always, but much alike. How many he had passed by before! But here he was this morning. It could not be merely that it was a fair, warm, summer's morning—hardly that. In his memory were a thousand other fair, warm mornings, with trees nodding outside the door and the blue sky beyond, and a voice as pleading and eyes as sad as these—almost. Whatever it was, this doctor, who examined a thousand immigrants a month, took a great deal of trouble to make it clear to Esther why it was her mother could not go.

"How can I tell her?" said Esther. "She cannot come, and yet we must go to Henry, who is waiting for us."

It was on the superintendent's hint that she told her mother that, though there was not money enough for all at that moment, she need not despair; for when they reached America she would have Henry send her ticket-money back.

The Emigrants

"Oh, my heart!" said Esther's mother, "and I must wait until that money comes again? You go now with the children, and not I? And yet it is right—it is right. Henry is impatient, and why not? The long time he has toiled for the tickets, and now he wishes to see his own. Esther, you are his own—and the children, little Michel and all. But not his wife's old mother? He will await every steamer now—go to the office and ask for Esther and the babies. Ah, ah, it is not right. No, I do not mean that. Esther, when you see him you will tell him, and surely he will manage to send the money soon. And yet it is so much to save—eighty rubles. One could live a long time at home on so much. But he is good, Henry, and he will not complain, and he shall see how I will make it up in care of the children. You and Henry, Esther, will have need of me. I will be taking care of the little ones when you help him at his work. But little Michel——"

Old Joseph stepped over. Timidly he plucked the superintendent by the arm. "I have enough —I will pay for Sarah's ticket." The pouch was in his hand, the string from around his neck.

"Sh-h—" said the superintendent, and told him how it was.

"Oh!" said old Joseph.

The Emigrants

But Esther's mother had caught sight of old Joseph, and divined what he had said. "Ah, Joseph, you will pay, and I shall not have to wait."

And then they had to tell her, or partly tell her —it was the sickness of the eyes.

"Even if we allowed you to leave here, old mother, they would send you back from New York. The American surgeons are very strict."

It took her some time to understand it. Her courage almost left her, and she had to sit down for a while; but, presently gaining a little strength, she inquired how long it would take the sickness to leave her. If she took good care, stayed in the darkened room, say, by the time Esther and her children arrived in New York and could send a letter back—would she be well then? Three weeks or more—four weeks it might be—five, possibly. Well, in five weeks—what a long time! but in five weeks would the sickness be cured?

Then it was that they told Esther the whole truth. Her mother's eyes would never be better. And Esther told Joseph, and Joseph led her away, with her fingers still clinging to little Michel's hand, and she still of the opinion that in a few weeks her eyes might be well and she on her way to join the children.

After that it was time for bathing. Every one must get under the stream of water and get such a wash as he never got before. They told Esther's mother that she could not go with the others, that she would have to give up little Michel because of the sickness of her eyes. In a little while, after they had been through the bath, little Michel would be brought back.

She protested at that. "So soon to lose him for long weeks, and now not to see him while he is washed?" So vehement was she that superintendent and surgeon threw up their hands and allowed her to have her way. So she took little Michel into the women's apartments and gave him so fine a warm bath, with such a plenty of soapsuds, that he crowed like a young rooster.

"Such a boy!" said Esther's mother, and held him up, rosy, for all to see, and later, with his glowing face, confronted the superintendent triumphant.

It was against all the rules that Esther's mother should go in the train for Hamburg. But she hung onto little Michel, to whom she was so soon to say good-by—hung on so tightly that when the train started the superintendent said something to the guard, and handed him a paper; the guard in reply said, "Very good—Berlin"; that and something else, and Esther's mother, happy and smiling, stayed aboard.

The Emigrants

Everybody in the car felt sorry for Esther's mother, and smiled at her and the baby when they saw that she had had her way.

All that night and all next morning they were confined to the rickety car, on the side of which, in large black letters, were the words,

RUSSISCHE AUSWANDERER

At times, along the way, there were stations where, the guard's vigilance relaxing, they might have had time to run out and procure needful things; but if their own guard were careless, not so the others, and they were soon rushed back. Everybody seemed to think that whoever else were accorded privileges, these lowly strangers at least should be given no liberty.

The young fellow, Moishe, he who had been to America before, explained how it was. "Some years ago some people—not our people, but others of Russia—carried the cholera into Hamburg and so on to America; and since then none are allowed to leave the cars until we are in Hamburg, and there we leave them only for the Auswanderer-hallen, and there it is lock and key also, until we shall be on the steamer. I know, for it was so when I went before also, although, upon my word, it seems harder now. Next time, should I come back again, I will return third class—no less."

19

The Emigrants

At Bromberg, which is well on toward Berlin, a boy having grapes for sale halted under the window of the car. "Ah!" sighed Esther, "if the babies had but a handful!" Old Joseph, hearing, leaned out, motioned for the full of his hat, and handed down a ruble. The boy shook his head.

"He will have none of your Russian money," said Moishe. "He wants German money. I remember that it was so before."

"But I have no German money," said poor Joseph, and was drawing in his head disconsolate when they were perceived by a young fellow whom they had themselves already noticed as one who seemed to have no other business than to walk the platform and observe the people about him. He was neither German nor Russian, they saw at once. To him, when he came over, Moishe handed Joseph's ruble and spoke some words in the strange tongue with which he used to converse with the superintendent at the control station when he wished to show that he had been to America.

The young stranger nodded, and for Joseph's ruble handed back German money. "Two marks and fifteen pfennigs"—they knew that much of German money; and then, stopping the fruit boy, he purchased the platter of grapes and handed it up to Esther's mother. Further, he ran off and came back with a precious orange for each of the children. Little Michel's hand was not large enough to hold his. "There," said Moishe proudly, "that is the American kind. Money, they have it like dirt to spend—these rich Americans. You will find them everywhere."

"Not many of them come to Poland," said old Joseph; "or, if so, I never saw them in our village."

Esther's mother fed the orange to little Michel. Between mouthfuls she hugged him tight, and in his ear whispered: "Ah, my little Michel, some day—who can say—you will also be rich, with money to spend like that; and with the money there will also be horses and carriages and grand houses and servants. And maybe I shall live to see it, and if so it may be that I shall be allowed there—in the grand house—in a little back room up under the roof with nobody to see me, but from where I can look and see all, knitting your socks for the bad weather and putting the letters on the fine linen you will have then. Is it not so, my little Michel?" and little Michel held his mouth up for more orange.

Not long after that it came to an end—at Berlin, where the train made a long halt. Esther's mother had almost forgotten that she was not to go, and was beginning to believe that she would yet be allowed to stay. But here was a new guard, one with less kindness than the other. He pulled out a paper and came through the car, calling loudly her name.

"Sarah—I cannot read it—but Sarah Something, an old woman." She had no cause to answer—the pitiful look that came to her worn old face would have made her known out of a multitude.

She pleaded with this one, even as she had with the doctor and superintendent, and up to the last moment hoped she might win him over. But this was one who dared not or could not go beyond orders—out of the car he lifted her as the train moved, out and onto the platform.

And after her came old Joseph. He had stopped not for bundles or boxes, but jumped off like a youth of twenty.

"You must tell her all," called Esther after him.

"I will tell her."

It was a most unheard-of thing, this leaving the car by one against whom no objection was made; and the astounded guard, with no precedent to help him out, was at a loss what to do. He gesticulated in bewilderment, but the train moved out.

Esther's mother did not see Joseph. She had eyes only for little Michel, with his arms reaching out of the window toward her, out over his mother's shoulder, as though for something he missed.

Long after the train was out of sight she stood there, despairing. Only when fatigue compelled her did she move to a bench, and then only to cast her weary body down and hold a tight hand to her aching eyes and head. Joseph, saying nothing, sat on another bench.

By and by the train that was to take her back to Russia came, and, arising, she saw him sitting there.

"You, Joseph? And why? Why, O Joseph, did you turn back, too?"

"Why? Why? As if you did not know. You in Poland and I stay in America? I am old, Sarah."

"And I am old, too, Joseph—so old, and never knew till now."

It was in the control station on the frontier that she was told the worst. It had to be told her. She had to be made to understand why it was that she was not to be allowed to stay there until the ticket should come from America—if all the tickets in the world were to come, still she could not go.

It was old Joseph who told her.

"So," she said, "so. Oh, you were a good boy. And Max, Jacob, Joseph—good children, all. And Esther, my daughter, you were good, too—Esther, yes. But Michel, O my heart! Oh, my little Michel——"

Then it was the tears came.

"That is better," said the surgeon. "But she will need care, old man, when she is back in Poland again—for all her days, it may be."

"She shall have care," said Joseph, "and for all her days, if need be."

Between the control station and their old home in Poland she spoke only once. Without lifting her head she reached out her hand.

"Joseph?"

"I am here."

"When the letters come from America it may be that my eyes—you heard what the doctor said?— my eyes—and in the letters may be things that are not for others to see— But I do not mind you, Joseph—and also there will be such things as little Michel will write when he grows up—you know, Joseph?"

"I know, Sarah."

"And so I may need eyes, Joseph. It is hard to say only that, to be only a burden to thee at the last, but I may need eyes, Joseph."

"Thou shalt have eyes, Sarah."

TSHUSHIMA STRAITS

Tshushima Straits

IT was the Russian battle-fleet steaming north-
erly toward the Sea of Japan. Twenty ships
were in column and ten miles an hour the speed.
From the quarter-deck of the *Kremlin* the American could hear the crew of the big turret at drill.
By the clanking echo of the tumbling tray he
could guess their speed.

He shook his head to himself. "No doubt
you're brave and all that, but you could stand an
awful lot of practice."

By and by, the loading tray no longer sounding, the form of a sailor emerged from the turret
hatch. A moment, as if to get his bearings,
another as if to take in the scene, and then in two
nervous bounds he made the deck.

The American knew him for his man, but he
finished his cigarette before stepping over to the
other's side. "Is not this Stephan Demetri Harlov so called, turret captain?"

"So called," the other replied in English, "so
called?" And then in French, "You speak a
strange tongue, m'sieur."

"Étranger? Eh bien, have it so," the American retorted in French. "You do not recall me?"

"Oh, yes, you are the American quartermaster we shipped at Hong-Kong."

"I am also an American naval officer on a leave of absence. My name is Mannix. I am that same young Mannix, the Annapolis cadet, who spent most of his furloughs in coming to see Her Grace's sister—before she became Her Grace, that was. Does M'sieur Harlov recollect?"

The Russian paused before answering, and then he spoke in English. "I recollect—very well. Ensign Mannix now, is it not? But you have changed."

"Naturally, of course—in seven years."

"And how is the pretty little Madeleine?"

"Quite well, thanks."

"Not Mrs. Mannix yet?"

"Not yet. And perhaps never. But she is concerned, and I am concerned, and her sister is concerned in what I have to say to you—if Stephan Demetri Harlov, enlisted man in His Imperial Majesty's navy, has a short half-hour to spare?"

"Some matters, Mr. Mannix—is it not best to let some matters rest?"

"Not this matter, Your Grace. To-morrow you fight, and to-morrow, possibly——"

"—I die?"

"Exactly."

"And why not you die also?"

"Exactly."

"And if I die and you die, how can it matter then?"

"It will not matter to us. But Her Grace——"

"Meaning?" There was a note of mockery in the Russian's voice.

"Meaning"— there was a note of stubbornness in the American's—"meaning Her Grace, Miss Madeleine's sister—my sister-in-law, possibly, if I return from my mission."

"Ah-h, a mission?"

"Exactly—a mission."

It was a night of drizzle with recurring fog, and they had been peering into each other's faces while talking. Now the Russian looked suddenly away. "What a scene for a drama!" he exclaimed. "See that taffrail plunging. The dripping deck beneath us—gleaming distantly. And outboard"— he swept his arm in half a circle— "profoundly dark, except where on the swirl of the tidal waters the sweeping search-lights play."

The Russian pointed to where astern was a towing spar on which three search-lights were concentrated; and listening and looking, Mannix began to appreciate the sensitive side of this man who could see, weigh, believe, and judge in an instant. "They make one think of mad porcupines charging like that, do they not?" And again the fog enveloping and the safety signal whistles sounding, "We make so much noise and display so many lights! But it will not come to-night. No, not to-night. For what fleet could preserve an effective battle-formation in this sea and tide and gloom? They would be shelling each other before they were done. And to-morow—to-morrow!" he laid a hand on the American's arm; "for to get through the straits without meeting Togo's fleet, we cannot expect that—nor wish it. No, no. And"—this under his breath almost—"there can be but one outcome. But let us go inside," and Mannix followed him to the turret, where the other switched on an electric light.

A short, hardy, immensely powerful-looking sailor leaped to his feet and stood to attention. "S-st!" hissed Harlov; but not until he had seen the American did the sailor relax.

"And now?" queried the Russian.

"And now," began Mannix, and in the most rapid and concise language of which he was master made it clear how it was that his companion had come to misunderstand. In this cause Mannix could be eloquent. The Russian was quick to see. His cynicism began to leave him. Mannix did not have to half explain things. "Yes, yes, go on. Yes, yes," the Russian kept repeating. "But it is almost incredible, nevertheless—a plot from the most dramatic stage almost. A man that I know as a friend—it is almost inconceivable."

"Yet it is true. I was with him when he died—in his own cabin. He sent for me. Dying, he wished to make amends. For years his wild passion had goaded him to the most ingenious schemes to win—pardon, but it is so—the love of Her Grace. He considered the battle half won when you doubted. But he did not know this American girl—a thousand like him could not have stirred her. Only he had to arrive at death's door to learn that. But once convinced, he went just as far the other way to make amends. It was his own idea, the death-bed confession which I drew up and he signed."

"What!"

"Yes, and before witnesses."

Two bells struck. Mannix stood up. "I must go, for at nine o'clock I was to report to my division officer. But here is the confession. Read it. And if you say, I will see you in the morning—if all goes well."

"Yes, yes, in the morning. Adieu."

The division officer was detained, and so Mannix was told to wait in the passageway for him. From where he stood he could look into the ward-room. Several officers were lounging there. One was ordering wine for himself and another, instructing the boy carefully as to the rare vintage. "A pretty duty," he observed to his companion, "an economic principle. If we do not drink it to-night, it will probably rest on the bottom of the sea to-morrow. And a pity that."

At this point an officer, a lieutenant, entered the ward-room. "You seem pleased at the prospect," he said reprovingly to the wine-drinker, laying a bundle on the table.

"No, no, no." The other smiled and raised a deprecating hand. "Not pleased, but the thought of the excitement, it does relieve the strain. But what have you there, Nicolas Osin?"

"It is a suit of clothes, and I am looking for a cord to tie them up."

"Clothes! Have you not your underclothes, and will they not be enough to swim in when the time comes?"

"No, no, a suit of clothes to dress properly—afterward. I shall stow these somewhere on the gun-deck, and afterward——"

"And how if there is no afterward? How if one of your guns blows up and you with it?"

"Ah-h," and Nicolas Osin shrugged his shoulders. "Then I shall will them to you."

Two or three laughed, and one by the pianola, who had stopped his playing to catch the retort, set the machine in motion again. It was a German pianola, and Mendelssohn's "Spring Song" that he was rolling out.

Three others were gathered at a table on the starboard side, while a fourth was playing solitaire under the centre cluster of incandescent lights. The officer with the bundle, by a gesture, indicated the solitaire player. "Look at him now!"

The solitaire player looked up. "Oh, well, it is you, Nicolas Osin, Vice-Admiral Misanthrope, cheer up." And fixing his eyes on the bundle of clothing, "You are wise, too, Nicolas Osin. To-morrow morning, when I go off watch, I will envelop myself in the newest of underclothing, even to new socks, all of silk. The doctor says that if one is dressed in clean underclothing the danger of blood-poisoning from a wound is much lessened. I should not like to die that way—by blood-poisoning."

"Doctors," said the officer at the pianola, "doctors give useful advice—sometimes."

"As to that," began the solitaire player, "I could tell you—" But did not, for just then one of the three officers of the starboard side began to unroll a plan of something.

"Ho there!" The solitaire player scooped his cards into one pile. "What have you there, Alexai Fatischeff? Plans of battle evolutions, devolutions, revolutions?"

"It is a plan of my estate."

"What a lucky man—to have an estate!"

"I shall be luckier if—" He did not finish.

"We shall all be lucky, my friend, if by this time to-morrow night——"

"You croaking frog you, shut up!" came from the two companions of Alexai Fatischeff. "Shut up and go to bed!"

An officer in dripping oil-clothes entered the room. A half-dozen questions assailed him at once. "Still foggy—yes. And choppy—a little. And the search-lights still playing? Yes. Only for the towing spars we should have run into each other a dozen times to-night. And the enemy? No telling, but our wireless operator has been picking up wireless messages regularly."

"Then to-morrow?"

"It looks like it," and he passed on.

Mannix's division officer came along then. "Ah-h," he spied Mannix, gave him some rapid instructions in the event of a battle on the morrow, and then dismissed him.

Tshushima Straits

Mannix's way out led past the quarters of the senior officers. Here some doors were opened, some closed; but there was a light shining out from all. And such occupants as he could see seemed very much occupied, either writing or overhauling the contents of their desks. On the room door of one of these, that of Lieutenant Pushkin, who had charge of the after-turret, Mannix knocked. Pushkin knew of Mannix's mission.

Following the invitation to enter, Mannix looked in. Pushkin was at his desk. He was writing furiously and did not look up.

"I came to wish you good luck in case there should not be too much time to-morrow," said Mannix.

"Thank you. It is good of you. And to you, also, good luck." He regarded Mannix kindly. "And is it all right with Stephan Demetri?"

"I think it will be. On the eve of a battle a man is more likely to forget his little ego. Only now I am worrying for him in the battle. But you are writing home?"

"Yes," and Pushkin smiled absently. "To my wife. And my little girl—fourteen years. A hard world, and so a little word to her and advice how to bring her up—in case, in case—you know."

"Of course. Good-night."

"Good-night."

Tshushima Straits

II

NEXT morning Mannix, walking the superstructure, heard a gentle, "My friend, I thank you." It was the sailor, Stephan Demetri, saluting him. "You have done me and mine a great service, and at great peril to yourself. Yes, great risk; for somewhere in that haze ahead of us an enemy, a brave, fanatically brave enemy is waiting. And has been waiting—for months, and not grown weary in the waiting. So it may be I shall not get another chance to speak with you. I have done my wife a great wrong. And I ask, should I die and you live, that you will tell her so."

"But you are not going to die. You will live to tell her yourself."

"No, no. I know our captain. And all ships which do not strike their colors will be sunk. We are not properly prepared for battle. But those of us who are to die will not regret it, if only our example shall not be lost."

"You must live. There is the little fellow also."

"Yes, yes, but all things must give way now to—" he pointed to the flag at the peak. "And now it is eight bells—battle stations in our turret. Adieu." He gripped Mannix's hand, saluted profoundly, and hurried down to the quarter-deck.

All the morning a haze hung over the sea. The wireless operator was still picking up cipher messages which, his judgment told him, could only come from ships not many miles away. The haze and these undecipherable messages bred a feeling of uneasiness.

At noon Mannix was called to the bridge and given the wheel; and no more than had hold of it than there emerged from out of the haze a long, fast-moving steamer. All the signal men in the fleet jumped to their long glasses, but while they were yet trying to distinguish her colors she disappeared. She could not have been more than four thousand yards away, and Mannix speculated on what would have happened to her if his own China squadron were involved. A challenge it would have been, and at once an explanation, or a seven-inch shell would then and there have ended her cruising days.

The haze thinned, with Mannix still at the wheel of the *Kremlin*, when they came into view. Up to the northward they were, and for them clearly no surprise. Almost before they were seen from the *Kremlin's* bridge they were swung into column, and headed westerly across the Russian course.

Tshushima Straits

The Russian flag-ship signalled a change of course. Ere yet he had done putting his wheel over, Mannix saw the enemy were changing to meet it, and having greater speed were more prompt in execution. Months on the way had the Russian fleet been; with grass growing on their bottoms and machinery not in the best of condition, they were out-manœuvred from the first.

From his station on the open bridge of the *Kremlin*, Mannix had a good view of everything ahead. He thrilled as he read the signal that broke the battle flags out. And out they floated. Men's nerves strained to snapping at the sight. They cheered with something of hysteria. The enemy followed: The sunburst of Japan, but nothing cheerful to that sun.

A shell came wide of the Russian battle-ship's bows. Another—still wide. The careless sighting shots of a confident foe they seemed. Another and another—nearer. The next struck close to the *Kremlin's* bow, throwing high a column of water which drenched some sailors on the forecastle of the flag-ship. They ducked and ran back laughing. The shell continued on, ricochetting, on to the next in line without exploding. Another came skipping by. A sailor threw a piece of coal after it. All who witnessed this laughed, and the laughter relieved the tension. Everybody on the bridge had a word or two to say then.

"I see nothing wonderful in their shooting," said one. "Ho, ho, they boasted it would be like breaking pipes in a shooting-gallery." Mannix recognized in him the officer of the pianola. He turned on Mannix. "They are reported to have some American gunners aboard some of their ships. What of that, you American?" He said it half in malice, half in fun.

"There was no American behind that, be sure of that, sir. Our apprentice boys straight from the training-ships could do better than that."

The Russian ships were painted black, the Japanese gray, a war gray. Everything gray— hulls, stacks, stays, tops, masts, bridges—every- thing. And those gray silhouettes were in one long single column, steaming, perhaps, fifteen knots; and with the turmoil of their wakes and the white masses at every bow, they gave one some- thing to think about. Even in a peaceful evolu- tion, a silent column of war-ships sliding rapidly past without fuss or noise—the rapid sliding of a score of great, grim, gray ships across the gray seascape, it is wonderfully impressive. Even in times of peace it is so, but now it was war! the destiny of two nations, perhaps of two great races, depending on the outcome.

What officers were on the bridge were viewing matters most calmly; but down in his heart Mannix, though he would not have uttered the thought to these Russians nor listened if another said as much to him, down in his heart the feeling would not be dislodged—before even the first shell burst that day these gray ships looked the masters. And making up his mind to that, Mannix breathed a prayer for Madeleine whom, he made up his mind then, he was never to see again.

After four hours at the wheel, and perhaps five minutes after those first fighting shots, Mannix was relieved, but with instructions to be within call. He descended to the chart bridge, one deck below, and there waited.

Now the Russians were capped. Every Japanese ship lay ready, with a whole broadside to the head of the Russian column. And at once the Japanese opened up. Every ship in that long, gray line opened up on the first four ships of the Russian line. Only those first four ships were within range of the Japanese. Mannix's ship was in that first four. It was a rain of metal. All about the sea was white-capped with the ricochetting shells. Had but one-quarter of them come aboard, the Russian leaders would all have been sunk in that first twenty minutes. But in that short time enough shells came aboard—without leaving the chart bridge Mannix could see that—enough to make a mess of steel partitions, enough to make splinters of most of the woodwork (which should long ago have been removed, but wasn't), enough to dismount several guns, to bowl over several gun crews. Mannix would have liked to run about the ship to observe better how the men were behaving, but he did not dare to get too far away in case they should need him at the wheel. But even from where he was he caught characteristic touches of the fighting Slav. Almost beneath him he saw a gunner stop, squint out of a gun-port to see what was doing, suck in his cheeks, say most thoughtfully, "Well, well, but this cannot last long—they will soon have no shells left at this rate, and then what will they do?"

But mostly the men said nothing, except to utter soft remarks to themselves. The work of the guns, of lifting the wounded out of the way, of making repairs, absorbed them. They looked neither one way nor the other, saw little except the shell which they had to hoist into the breech, or the breech-block which they had to crank home, or the enemy's ships through the long-sighting telescope. There were men who paused helplessly in the very height of all this, probably

peasants who at the last moment had been driven
aboard. Some of these had never seen a ship of
the kind until that day when they had come over
the gangplank at Libau. One of these looked up
and, seeing the eyes of Mannix fixed kindly on
him—a gun was disabled and the crew were trying
to make the necessary repairs—he paused to say,
"If yon was a horse, or a cow, or a sheep now, I
could show you how to doctor him."

An officer called down to Mannix and sent him
off with a message to the chief of the powder division. From that Mannix guessed that the internal
communications had been shot away, and also
that many of the messenger boys had been killed
off. Down between decks he met with a few
skulkers in the passageways, waiting, no doubt,
for the battle to end. Some ugly stories had been
set afloat before the fight, and, no doubt of it,
there were many mutineers in that crew. Mannix found his powder-division officer. He was
the same who had been playing solitaire in the
ward-room the night before. When Mannix came
upon him he was calmly shooting down one of
these mutineers in an ammunition passageway.
The man did not even cry out as he crumpled up,
and the others there hardly looked at him. They
had not time, and besides, as one observed, he
deserved it.

Tshushima Straits

On his way back Mannix saw that it was going hard with his ship. The gunners, they meant well, but they did not know how. It was true that most of the Jap shells went wide too, but they were pumping them out so fast that if but one in ten found a mark it was enough. Mannix saw that one shell was jammed in a port on the gun-deck and two plates were torn away from her forward; above the water-line, it was true, and no great danger from that yet because of the smoothness of the sea, but if the ship should list toward that side! There were holes in smoke-stacks—several; but as yet only one showed signs of toppling over.

Mannix caught a flying rumor of a hole below her water-line aft, and also of an explosion in the after-turret magazine. This was the Duke's turret. He wanted to rush aft to find out more about it, but felt he might be needed on the bridge. And he was. The helmsman had just been killed. His blood was yet on the spokes, making them difficult to grasp. Mannix was busy for a few minutes rubbing first one hand and then the other against his blouse, to clear them of the blood.

The enemy, having successfully completed their first manœuvre, were now about to attempt a loop about the entire Russian fleet. They went about it in a superbly insolent manner, as if what the Russians did could not matter. Mannix said to himself, "God! there's a fleet I know of that you couldn't try that on and get away with it!" Possibly he said it aloud, or showed by his expression what he was thinking of, for an officer, the pianola-player, turned and smiled on him.

The next instant the entire port side of the bridge caved in. Also the steering-gear was parted. "You are out of a job," said the pianola-player. An instant later he was struck with a shell. "And I also!" he added, and lay still. Mannix looked and saw that the stanchions supporting the bridge had been shot away on one side. Shells were whistling through all the free space on the bridge. "Some qualified gun-pointer has got the range of this place," thought Mannix, and was about to find a new post when he felt a dull blow in the side. It was not painful, and he could not understand why he went down. He was puzzling that out when he was almost overcome by a feeling of nausea. It was difficult for him to keep from vomiting. And the funny thing was that he had had nothing to eat since breakfast. He may have lost consciousness, or he may have merely lost track of time, but certainly the next notice he took was of himself being on the forward end of the forecastle head and looking up at the bridge-works, which had collapsed and were burning. "Queer that," thought Mannix, and, though he did not know why he did it, climbed up on the forward turret where was a man on his knees. He was gazing down into the turret, that officer. Mannix knelt beside him. "What do you think?" he said to Mannix, and pointed inside. Mannix looked. Every man there was dead. It must have been instant incineration with all of them. Bodies there that if a hand were but laid upon them would have crumbled like the dust they were. Charred to ashes these, but with the outlines of the forms perfectly preserved.

Mannix took another look. On the casemate, not a mark; of the guns, no displacement. This was the only man of all that turret crew who had been left alive. He had been sent off with a message, and had only got his head into the under-hatch on his return when the shell struck. He seemed hard of hearing and very much astonished. "Why, I felt nothing, Your Excellency, absolutely nothing. But it was terribly—O terribly hot!" he added. "And what shall I do now, I wonder?" He repeated that last, "What shall I do?" several times.

Mannix suddenly found himself wondering why it was he felt no horror. But so it was. He was like a man on the side-lines watching some game, but much less wrought up than if it were the—the annual game between the army and the navy say.

Thinking to get word of the Duke, Mannix went aft. Treading his way through the débris of the gun-deck, he saw that half the port battery had been put out of commission. "And the fight not yet half over," he thought. Blood was not yet everywhere, but there was already more than was pleasant to see or smell. Wounded men were being taken below to the hospital; but there were too many for the hospital corps, and so here and there were groups attending to themselves. Bandaging each other they were mostly. They were rather serious, but not too much so. That it was a great battle they were engaged in seemed not to have any intellectual interest for them. They were wounded, that was all. Some were gone beyond hope and knew it. "Ah-h, if I had but a samovar now, I would make me a fine last cup of tea," said one in a wistful voice. Mannix saw another with his back to a bulkhead, his legs stretched out before him, rolling a cigarette. Having only one arm left, he was having difficulty. He hailed Mannix, otherwise Mannix would never have known; for, bareheaded, blackened, stripped to his undershirt, there was no mark or rank to distinguish him from any enlisted man. Mannix turned back at the call, and saw that it was the officer who had been tying up his clothes the evening before, he who had been called Nicolas Osin. "I shall not need them after all. If you want them—we know of you—they are there," and he nodded his head toward a wooden chest which, in some way, had escaped demolition.

"But you are far from being dead," exclaimed Mannix. "One arm, what is that?"

"One arm?" Nicolas Osin smiled, almost proudly. "One arm, indeed. If you should turn me over now, you would see a hole as big as your whole head, so they tell me. A piece of shell, yes, and a marvel it did not come clear through. Most surprising, yes, how those shells act." He puffed at his cigarette.

"And Sergei Herzar, he is gone, yes. Ps-s-t!" —he made an upward movement of his arm— "like that. And not so much as a button for a souvenir. Only this morning at breakfast he was speaking to me of a letter to his wife, and was much worried that she might not get it. There was a little estrangement before he left home, and he was asking forgiveness now, and now she will never know; for the mail-box, of course, will sink with us. Oh, she will be sunk, there is no doubt of it. Our captain is one who will never strike his colors."

"The captain is dead," said Mannix.

"So? Too bad. But no matter, the *Kremlin's* colors they will not be struck. But go on about your business. Suffer? Oh, no, no! But I am going, of course. Adieu."

Mannix rushed on to Pushkin's room, which was on the deck below. In a hundred ways the ship was now showing that she was hard hit. She would not much longer remain afloat, and Mannix wished to save a few little things which Pushkin had allowed him to stow away in his desk; that is, if he saved himself. He could hardly get through the ward-room, it was so cluttered with wreckage. Two holes gaped in the starboard side. Not one thing had been left whole. The keys of the German pianola were scattered all over the deck. The place was full of smoke, gas, vapor; a vapor that made it difficult and dangerous to take in even the quickest breath. Mannix rushed through to his room, snatched Madeleine's packet of letters from a drawer, belted on a revolver he saw hanging up, and came away.

The after-ladder to the quarter-deck had become impassable. He had to go clear amidships to find a ladder to the deck. There was a man at the foot of the ladder. He was coughing weakly. Mannix stopped to ask him his trouble.

"No, I am all right now, but down there"—he pointed below—"are many, many suffocated, the entire powder division—the gas from their accursed shells."

Mannix reached the quarter-deck. There they were still fighting the after-turret, irregularly, as if not many of the crew were left. Mannix dropped into the turret. The Duke was there, leaning against the casemate, wounded. Mannix asked after Pushkin. The Duke pointed to a body. "Dead?" asked Mannix. The Duke nodded. They had not enough men to work the guns. One gun lacked both a trainer and a pointer. Mannix stepped up to the gun-pointer's telescope. He had had no serious intention of doing this, but now he could not help it. He turned to the Duke. "With your permission?" he said. "Help yourself," said the Duke pleasantly.

Mannix almost shouted with exultation as he fired. No strange work was this for him. On his own gun-ship he had been a turret officer. That first shot went to the mark. And the next. And then he heard from behind. "She's going now, surely. It is the boilers—they have blown up!"

"Leave—at once—everybody!" commanded the Duke.

There was still a shell in the chamber of Mannix's gun. "We may as well fire this one," suggested Mannix.

"By all means," replied the Duke.

Mannix, after looking back to make sure the breech-block was closed, pointed and fired. He saw a great commotion when it landed. "A bull's-eye!" cried the one man who had stayed behind to see the effect. That man also stooped to raise the Duke in his arms. Only Mannix, the Duke, and this man were left in the turret. The Duke was helpless. It was his legs, both legs. "Ivan, get out—quick!" commanded the Duke.

"Yes, Your Grace, but with you," said Ivan.

"Come," urged Mannix, "she is sinking, and you must try to help yourself."

"No, no. I will go down with her. I should not want to live after she is gone. But you must go. You are the kind that women love. You will win Madeleine, have no fear."

"But your wife?"

"What of her?"

"You believe in her?"

"Ah-h, but what does she think of me?"

Mannix looked at Ivan, who saluted and lifted the Duke through the under-hatch and onto the quarter-deck. The ship was now to the gun-deck and lurching. The quarter-deck would soon be under. Mannix wondered what he could get that would float a man's body. Over by the ward-room hatch he spied a table, or what was left of it unburned, floating up from beneath. He was not sure that he could pull it through to the deck, but he tried. A half-burned leg broke off, then another, and then, Ivan rushing over and taking hold, it came through. There was also another table, with some parts of the German pianola and the wreck of a chair.

Mannix and Ivan lashed the two table-tops together with strips of the table-cloth. They had now only to let them slide down from the steeply inclined deck to the ship's side. They lifted the Duke, who was but half conscious, and laid him across the table-top. It held him up without trouble. Mannix took hold of the chair for himself, but seeing a sailor looking at it wistfully, he asked, "Can you swim?"

"No, Your Excellency."

"Then take it."

"Thanks to Your Excellency," and plunged into the sea with it.

"But you, Ivan," asked Mannix, "can you swim?"

"Swim? I? If I was rated by my swimming and not by my brains, I, Your Excellency, would be flying an admiral's stars."

"Shove off, then!" ordered Mannix.

They were barely clear of the ship when she started her death-rolling. She was a monstrous sight in that final roll, with one bilge keel and a propeller up-pointing and the smoke pointing from her. And the flames flashing through the smoke. A great volume of steam up-rushed as the burning hull went under. Mannix looked about. Only the Duke, Ivan, himself, and that other sailor to whom he had given the chair seemed to have come safe away from the *Kremlin*.

III

MANNIX now felt the sting of a wound in his right side and another in the left thigh. It seemed to come to him dimly that he had felt these before, ages before. No doubt it happened at about the time the bridge was demolished. Only for the salt-water, which made his wounds smart, probably he would not have noticed them now. It was painful for him to work his arms and legs, but yet he must if he was to get anywhere with the Russian who, lying helpless and heedless across the table, seemed not to care whether he lived or died. "But I care!" thought Mannix. "No reason in the world why I should die too. Sorry though I am for Russia, still she is not my country, and I have something else to hope for."

With the palm of one hand resting on the edge of the table, Mannix found he could easily keep afloat, and by kicking out with his sound leg he saw that he could steer the little raft toward several straying ship's boats. Just before the action began some of the ships had cast away their boats, and now there was a string of half a dozen —gigs, whale-boats, sailing cutters—drifting about to windward and not too far away.

The haze had gone entirely now and the sun shone clear; a low sun, for it was getting late in the afternoon. Mannix seized a chance to count the fleet. One other was gone besides the *Kremlin*, and two others looked as if they had not long to remain afloat. Hopelessly shot through these two were, and through the holes near the water-line the sea was pushing. Scorched and blistered they were, with here and there the steel plates melted into horrible-looking bunches. All this, with huge clouds of smoke and darting tongues of flame, made terrible sights of them.

As Mannix looked he saw a Russian destroyer range alongside the flag-ship. He guessed they were taking off the body of the Admiral, the limp body was handled with such extreme care. There was no sea on, but the long, oily roll broke against the body of the big battle-ship and, resurging, lifted the little destroyer, now high up, and again let her sag away down. She looked, that once imposing battle-ship, like an old tramp steamer that had been lying for years on some beach till somebody happened to remember that she would make a good target for the fleet at target practice, and so they had taken her out and shot her up. Mannix marvelled that she was still afloat.

At this point the Duke cried out. Mannix turned his head. The Russian was struggling to lift himself to his elbow to see the flag-ship more clearly. "A pity—a brave man, our Admiral," he said after a moment of observation, and then Mannix thought he heard him sob.

Mannix could count dozens of small pieces of wreckage. These, being on a level with his eyes, loomed up like little hills on a level plain. Floating in the water, clinging precariously as they were to these bits of wreckage, were a few surviving sailors of the fleet. As they labored and struggled to get on, a destroyer of the enemy came tearing by. Her swash washed several of them into the sea. Most of the destroyer's crew seemed to be on deck, on their faces triumphant smiles. One called out and, leaning over the life-line, laughed and pointed, then threw what looked like a piece of exploded shell at one of these swimming sailors. It did not strike the swimmer, who, looking over his shoulder and seeing whence it came, hurriedly submerged himself. Evidently they wanted to have a little fun with him, for they ran close to him, as if trying to see how close they could come without actually running over him. Mannix happened to remember then: Why, this was the Duke's man, Ivan. His revolver lay on the table beside the Duke. He took it up, thinking to shoot one of them, but the destroyer was steaming perhaps twenty-five knots an hour, and in the middle of the swirl under her quarter as she turned was the Russian sailor. Mannix thought he was gone, but he was a tough one, and when the destroyer and her grinning crew had passed on he bobbed up.

"Was it not true, what I told Your Excellency, that I could swim well?" he said smilingly, as he came up hand over hand.

They reached one of the drifting boats. Ivan lifted in his master, and then helped Mannix, after which there came a dull explosion. "A torpedo," said the sailor sententiously. "Look, Your Excellency—the *Bovodino*." Mannix saw it, and the sight made him think of a death-stricken whale. Heavily, slowly, from one side to the other, the great war-ship rolled. And then, solemnly, completely over and forever from sight.

Mannix heard the sound of a screw behind him. It was the Japanese destroyer again. A voice hailed, but he made no answer. She drew up and stopped her engines not fifty feet away. An officer was sitting on a camp-chair on the side nearest to them. One elbow rested on the top life-line, and in the hand of that arm, between two fingers, he held a cigar. His other elbow rested on his knee, and that hand supported his chin. The very way he held the cigar and stared, it was unbearably insolent. Not a word did he say, just stared at the shipwrecked group. Mannix thought he smiled. "Beast!" said the Duke, and, raising himself on this thwart, returned with an even more insolent expression his enemy's stare. The two remained staring across so, each with all the insolence and contempt he could master. Suddenly the Jap called out something short, sharp, and in Russian. Mannix could not get what it was. "Oh!" cried the sailor. "Oh, to Your Grace!" and sank back.

The Jap slowly placed his cigar between his lips and puffed, blew the smoke toward them, and smiled. Mannix could just see that smile in the gloom. "Pardon," said the Duke, and, taking Mannix's revolver, fired.

The Jap made as if to stand up, and did half stand up for an instant. Then his body took a forward lurch, sagged the life-line half to the deck, and pitched forward and overboard. With the splash of the body the sailor seized the Duke and dropped overboard. "Come, Your Excellency," he whispered to Mannix, and made for an over-turned boat which Mannix had not before no-ticed. The next in line it was, with a plank torn out near the keel. Mannix followed the sailor and helped him with the Duke. "I can use my arms but not my legs," whispered the Duke. "Now, Your Excellency," called out the sailor, and Mannix, sinking beneath the water, followed the sailor beneath the gunnel of the overturned boat.

Between the surface of the water and the bot-tom of the overturned boat was room and air for twenty men to bob around and breathe in. They had only to hang onto a thwart to keep them-selves afloat. The boat which they had just left prevented them from seeing what was doing aboard the destroyer; but now an explosion almost made their upturned boat jump clear of the water. Mannix looked through the hole near the keel. The destroyer's people were shooting at the boat they had just left. Another shell and there was nothing left of it. Another shell, possibly to make sure, and then the destroyer steamed back and forth, as if looking to see if any had survived.

They watched her steam off in the last of the daylight, to make sure she had gone. That was just after sunset in the twilight, the sun going down in a burning glow that night.

"We cannot stay here," said Mannix.

"No, Your Excellency. In two minutes I shall be back," and the sailor disappeared. Soon he was alongside again with a free boat. Between them, Mannix and the sailor, they tore a few more planks from the bottom of the capsized boat, and lifted the Duke through. It was hard work, and when it was done all three again lay flat on their backs and studied the stars.

It was the sailor who moved first. Without being ordered, he stepped and stayed the mast, shipped the rudder, and hoisted the two sails.

"A useful chap, this sailor," commented Mannix. "Who is he?"

"He is from my estate. For hundreds of years his ancestors were the serfs of my ancestors, but to-day the serf is a better man than his master."

"Better than either of us," added Mannix. "And now we should get away. It might not be well for us to be found here in the morning—by our friends from that destroyer, for instance."

"Tell Ivan what you wish. He is of iron and can go without sleep for a week."

Tshushima Straits

Mannix gave the sailor the tiller, pointed to a star in the south, and the cutter began to slip through the darkness. And such a darkness! The fires from the burning Russian battle-ships only accented it.

For hours the Russian sat on a thwart and looked out on the dark sea without a word. At last he turned to Mannix. "The black night of Russia. But not our fault. Nor the navy's fault. No, no. Officers and men, we know how to fight. But when we have in power bureaucrats, politicians, who love their country only for what they can squeeze from that country, what is to be expected? Such as he"—pointing to Ivan at the tiller—"you see how he fights when he is loyal. And when he is not loyal, who is to blame?" He turned away, and Mannix fancied he was crying to himself.

"Shall we go home, Your Grace?" Mannix asked at last.

"Ah-h!" he sighed, "it is too much to hope for."

They sailed on, and all went well with them thereafter.

THE CONSUMING FLAME

The Consuming Flame

THERE was a boarding-house in San Francisco—the roof could be seen from the tops of a ship in the stream, and frequented mostly by ship captains it was; a great place, with Mrs. Mangan always there to put the good heart into everybody.

A fine old lady, Mrs. Mangan, and the prettiest girl, they say, when she married Mangan. A notably quiet man, Mangan, except for the twice a year or so when he exploded in the grand spree which kept his vessel in port for an extra week or two. But he was lost at sea, leaving a son, Bat, who grew up into one of the dare-devil skippers of the West coast. Not a port from Magellan to Behring Sea that didn't have a story of Bat. A wild one, but great-hearted too, who made and spent a half-dozen fortunes in his time, and came home one day with a beautiful Chilian wife—not so very long this before he was lost. A foolish thing, but he said he was going to make a port that night. Gale or no gale, he would—he'd come to moorings; and so he did—and took all hands with him.

The Consuming Flame

He left a little baby girl, which old Mrs. Mangan took care of, for the Chilian wife did not live long after Bat was lost; and Chiquita, her father's baby name clinging, grew up, and was so pretty growing up that the boarders went daft about her, and spoilt her, naturally, as such men will. Great men of their kind, who gave—and took—easily.

Jack Gateley came to know her while she was still little, because the house they lived in was owned by his father. Later, after the death of Jack's father, who drank himself straight into the grave when Jack's mother died, old Mrs. Mangan used to call him in to give him cookies; and, of course, any boy would like to be asked in there to see the big ship captains, and hear them tell of the strange places they had been to. And the talk of these wide-sailing ship-masters got into Jack's blood so that he enlisted in the Navy to see the world, and when he came back from his first apprentice cruise the beauty of Chick Mangan burst on him like a night shell on the target range. A flame of color and warmth it was; and not to Jack alone. On the street hardly a man passed—and women, too—but turned to look again. Perhaps the women, too, were not unaware of him. It used to make Jack quiver just to sit near her; and when she kissed him, that trembled even at the thought of it, and of her own accord —the two alone in her grandmother's parlor the day he was to sail again—it was like a torch to his soul.

And straight from that to the China station he went and put in three years there, regularly getting letters from her; scrawly letters, and neither could she spell the commonest words; but more to make his heart jump in a dozen lines than in all the books of poetry the ship's library held. And he used to write her long letters, too; and not a thing he saw in the East but he would wonder what she would think or say of it; not a thing he bought but he wondered would she like it; and for weeks before he got his discharge he thought of but little else but how she would look and act—would she kiss him again?—and he was all of a-tremble coming up the street from the dock, and arriving at the door of the old boarding-house he was gasping like a man who had just run a long race.

"She's upstairs somewhere," said Grannie Mangan, when she had done crying over Jack, and he went up to find her.

He could hear her little church organ, imagined her as knowing that his ship was in and waiting for him in the same old parlor alone, and so he did not knock. But she was not alone, did not hear the door turn. It was a steamer captain with her, Prady, who was said to make much more out of smuggling silks, opium, Chinamen, one thing and another, many times what his captain's pay amounted to. Prady, sidewise to the doors, was bending over her. She stopped playing. "Chick," murmured Prady, and kissed her—and she let him. The note in Prady's voice made Jack's heart grip small within him, and he backed out and drew the door to, but now not without being heard. Prady's challenging voice called out, "Who's there?" and Jack, having it in his mind to beat up Prady, re-entered; but, seeing her, he forgot.

"Jack—Jack—oh, Jackie, but the man you've grown to be!"

"Yes, and the woman you've grown to be!"

She misunderstood, and such a smile that, had it lasted, Jack could not have held out; but, greeting his eyes fairly, she could not fail to understand. Such bewilderment, such shame to her. "Oh, Jackie!"

"'Oh, Jackie!'" he mimicked her cruelly. "And so you've struck your colors, Chick—my colors, too. And your letters—were they nothing but to blind me? How long has it been going on?"

She shrank away from him.

The Consuming Flame

It had all happened so quickly. She stood up when she heard the door close behind him. "Oh, Jackie, Jackie! But I wasn't bad! no, not bad, Jackie—don't think that!" but he was gone, running up the street.

Whatever Prady may have thought and done before, he thought and did the right thing now. "Look here, Chick, I see where that lad didn't get things right. What'll I do? Say it—anything to make it right. Anything, I say—and that means anything, not barrin' death."

"Oh, go away—go away."

II

THAT night Jack Gateley got drunk for the first time in his life, and everybody knew it next day. Chick sent for Prady and he went out to find Jack, and, locating him, came back to Chick. "Go back there," ordered Chick. "I'll follow you."

Prady went in and pleaded with him, as well as he could with so many within hearing. But no use: the lad was just the age. All the stories that ever he heard from fo'c's'le rovers were sounding in his ears, and their one moral borne out. Women! women! huh! He himself had not patrolled the far ports without knowing something of that. And from such surprising quarters! And not alone from those who had the name of it. What he did not appreciate was that swinging down the street in power and straightness and beauty, with his head and face and bearing, he was a figure to focus wandering eyes. But it did come at times from such surprising quarters! What might have happened to him could surely have happened to others, as others had said, and not alone from those who had the name of it.

If the flooding tide of idealism had hitherto borne him in high, clean waters, so now its ebbing had left him on murky, wreck-marked shores. And Prady was the last man to influence him now. Prady! He recollected now that on his way up from the dock the day before he had met an old chum who had said, "Know this Captain Prady? Well, he calls around there pretty often, he does." No more than that, but enough now, remembering what he had seen and what he had had in mind. Since that day before he had been wondering what weakness possessed him not to beat this man up. So now he flouted Prady, and Prady, not overtrained to deference, had to talk back to some extent. Enough. Hardly time for Prady to guard, after the word passed, before Gateley was on him. A powerful man, Prady, and wily as a serpent, but this boy could have battled toe to toe with the great John L. himself and made him break ground that night. He smothered Prady, hit him so fast and often that before the other well knew he was fighting at all he was beaten. From the corner Jack dragged him across the room, hove him through the swinging doors and out into the street.

Prady, who came then as near to achieving heroism as a man in his position might, picked himself up, and, bleeding and dishevelled, carried the word to the waiting Chick. "And you wouldn't expect me to hang around after that, would you, Chick?"

She, who had caught intermittent glimpses of it through the window, was thinking more of Jack than of Prady. What a man he had grown to be! "No, Captain," she said, "I'll wait myself now. Good-night."

And she waited. Lurking like an outcast in the shadows, with patrolling policemen and the passing throng viewing her shrinking figure speculatively, she waited. She meant to speak to him. She would speak, and his companions, whatever sort of men they might be, could think what they pleased. And he came out at last and she stepped forth—but she did not speak. No man, but a woman! Poor Chick shrank back, but not before the woman had seen her—and laughed at her. 'Twas plain enough, a discarded acquaintance of her handsome sailor's. And not so bad-looking, and a figure! She laughed again, and this time Jack took notice. He saw a woman's figure shrink into the doorway, knew not what kind she was, only that here was another woman jeering at her. He stopped. "Here," he said, and from a thick roll gave her a large bill. "Good-night."

The girl eyed him and eyed the roll. He was good to look at, and he surely carried a lot of money with him. "W-why—what's the matter?"

"Nothing. Don't feel bad now—you're all right—but good-night."

Chick from her doorway saw the parting; and even better than he himself, or the girl, understood what it meant; and the tears came to her eyes, and she not one who cried easily. She saw him then continue his way, entering a street that led toward her home. In wild hope she followed, only to see him stop before the door of what had been once his home, but long sold to Charlie Wing.

She knew of this Charlie Wing, as who had not? And suspected more than she knew. Seldom did she go out but Charlie Wing passed her before she reached home again. She could not say why, but she had a dread of Charlie Wing. With the door of Wing's place closed behind Jack Gateley,

The Consuming Flame

Chick ran around to her own grandmother's, which was on the opposite side of the same block, and there was Captain Lappen.

As wild a fellow, Dan Lappen, as ever beat through the Golden Gate; whose one hope for years had been, but almost given up now, to marry Chick Mangan. In his mind—part idealist and part plain pirate—ran a vague notion of some day doing a deed that would bring her to her knees in admiration of him.

It was Lappen who once stood on the steps of her grandmother's boarding-house after a successful cruise, with a bundle of new five-dollar bills in the open palm of his hand, and blew them off, one by one, and "Lord in heaven! see 'em sail," kept saying while the wind was floating them down the street.

Foolish? Maybe; but it was Chick Mangan looking at him from behind the curtains, only fourteen years old this time, but tall, rounded, overpowering in her beauty even then, and thinking him a wonder for it. Lappen wouldn't have mourned a million five-dollar bills that day, for after it he performed the most thrilling deed of all his life—a kiss stolen from Chick, a memory cherished in secret.

The witchery of the girl had never left this free-booter of the sea. "Some day you'll be marryin',

I s'pose, Chick?" he said to her now after some desultory conversation, as he had a hundred times before in just that tone, and she answered in the same old words, "Surely, some day," only now without the smile or the blush.

"And what kind of a man?"

"Oh-h—" Poor Chick was worn out, unprepared for catechising. "Oh-h—a man with lots of money, I suppose."

She had never said that before, and Lappen leaped up. "Then I'll make the money:

"Oh-ho, we'll sail in the morn
For the Golden Horn—
Oh, the treasure pirates' bay—
And we'll strike 'em aboard
And we'll crimp their hoard
And sink 'em where they lay."

He danced a few steps in time to show how merry he felt. "Oh, those were the days, Chick!" and a wistfulness almost tremulous in his voice.

Chick laughed; and it pleased him to make her laugh. "I'll sail in the mornin', to make a fortune for Chick Mangan." Chick, staring absently at him, thought of something. All the men in the world had become fit for but one purpose. "You can do better than to make money, Captain—to please me?"

The Consuming Flame

"Name it, Chick."

"You know Jack Gateley?"

"Jack Gateley's boy, that died—that used to sit around here by the hour and never a word but listenin' to what everybody was sayin'—that little fellow?"

"Yes, but a big fellow now. And you know Charlie Wing's?"

Lappen knew Charlie Wing's, where the silk store was on the lower floor and the upper floors given over to gambling. And he knew Charlie Wing. Quite a man in his way, this Wing, who made a lot of money and spent all he made; said to be one-quarter Chinese, but liking not to be reminded of it. No cringing Chinese laundryman type, but of fine large presence and large ways; a splendid dresser, perhaps too splendid a dresser —his finger-rings alone must have stood him tens of thousands. But Chick was speaking.

"I want you to get him out of there. You knew his father, his mother—and the great kind they were—he's the last of his people. A pity if he went wrong. Get hold of him, Captain. For God's sake, Captain, get him away—away from doing wrong till he comes to himself."

So Lappen, docile as Prady was, went and found him. Even while Lappen stood by, Jack lost a year's rent of his father's houses, and Lappen, standing by, also saw Charlie Wing offer Jack his whole pile back.

The young fellow's eyes narrowed. "Why?"

"I knew your father," said Charlie.

"A good many people knew my father. Some he'd better not known. That money? Not much; but I'll take a cigar," and did, from off the side-board, and lit up and went on, "because I feel I'm entitled to it, like any other customer," and snapped the burnt match across the room, and Lappen noticed that it went where he had aimed it—plumb centre into the silver-mounted cuspidor.

"No use temptin' that lad with promises o' money-makin'," thought Lappen. "His kind, it's excitement they want—to forget things," and wooed him instead with hints of desperate adventure, and won him in the end. And at dawn they sailed out through the Golden Gate, with never a notion of when they were coming back.

Across the Pacific, the length and the breadth of the sealing country, from the Japan coast clear on around, they cruised. They raided rookeries and they raided the wide sea. Wherever were any seals, season or no season, law or no law, they hunted them. They were not alone at it, for Japs and Russians and a few from British Columbia were there; but it was taking big chances, for all four nations— Japan, Russia, England, and their own country—had war-ships there to see that the rookeries were protected and the pelagic laws observed.

And the two men grew to know each other, and Lappen to like the other rarely, as Chick Mangan well knew he would. And Lappen, who meant originally to make use of Jack to further his own interest with Chick Mangan, gave over the notion. Talking with the young fellow, pumping his very soul as they walked the deck on quiet evenings, the lad revealed himself, and Lappen came to have a higher notion of many things. He had broken his promise to keep the boy from wrong; but he would bring him home and give her the money he had gathered so that she could hold her head up—no pauper—if ever she married this lad. Lord, what was money to him? And hadn't he sailed, as a boy, with great Bat Mangan, her father, who'd 've given him his shirt? Perhaps she would refuse to take it, but at least she would stand off and say, "Well, Dan Lappen, you're sure something of a man!" and maybe kiss him on her wedding day. And this cruise over, he would never again run against the law—never.

The *Hattie Rymish* was chased a dozen times, and forced to lay in hiding after each chase till it was safe to try again. Lappen had, during this time, converted a good many seal-skins into gold

—English, American, and Russian gold pieces. "In case anything happens to me, I want you to bring that money home to Chick," he would say to Jack. Even should he get caught or killed he made Jack promise he would tell her what chances he took to get it. "She'll like that," he said.

"A good pile there now," he said one day, "but it will be twice that before the year's out." And so it would have, long before that year was out, if he had not grown over-bold. It was off Saghalien Island and a Jap cruiser; not three months before this an American gun-boat had killed half a dozen Japs for just what they had done a dozen times.

Their chance now was to run in and tuck behind the rocks somewhere. Twenty miles or so ahead of them was a goodly place. A boat was lowered over the side and the men told to row ashore—no more than a quarter of a mile. By and by the vessel would drop back and pick them up.

Lappen and Jack, by staying aboard, hoped to save the vessel; and they did get her almost into the cove, with everything ready for getting away quickly, but the cruiser had her long-reaching rifles and, while yet four thousand yards away, she opened up on the schooner; and it is a pretty big shell, a three-inch, to be tearing up the water

The Consuming Flame

alongside a little wooden hull. The *Hattie* wasn't too easy to hit, they having put her end-to, making a narrow enough target of her; but in time something was bound to come aboard; and one shell did, taking the main-mast ten feet above the deck and scattering pine splinters everywhere, big flying billets that came nigh to killing them both. Close enough that, and Jack made ready the boat to row ashore while Lappen ran below to get his bags of gold.

"Oh, we shot away her mizzen and we shot away her
    fore,
And 'Quarter! quarter!' cried they, as o'er the rail we
    bore.
But the quarter that we gave them was the bottom of
    the sea,
A-sailin' down the coast of the High Sag-a-lee,"

carolled Lappen. "And God! but when I get that back to 'Frisco, there'll be money enough for her—and a story to tell her!"

And so it would have, but that he had to pry open his state-room door, which was swollen, and was still tugging at the door when a shell came through the stern, straight on through the cabin, through the after bulkhead, and exploded somewhere in the main-hold. There was no need to tug at the door then; it flew open and with it almost half the vessel's side. The water rushed

77

into her so fast that in no time Lappen was standing to his knees. But the closet door within the state-room still stuck. "Come on," yelled Jack from deck; "never mind the money!"

"No, no!" cried Lappen; "it's for Chick!" and Jack heard the smash of his boot driving through the splintering wood. Jack was holding the bow of the boat to the vessel's side, all ready for a quick leap. "Hurry, hurry—for God's sake, hurry!" he cried.

"Coming!" Lappen called out, and then it was that a shell caught her below the water-line and lifted her—her whole after-end. For perhaps a second Jack saw him. He must have got to the top of the cabin-ladder; in one last great effort he must have hoisted the two bags of gold high over his head, for they showed clear of the water, the hands and two wrists under them— no more than that—and down again in the last rush of the smothered vessel.

Jack jumped into the boat and drove her aft. He did not have to go clear astern, but rowed her straight over what was left of the quarter-rail, even then well under water. He looked down. He could see nothing; but thinking that Lappen might be tangled in the main-sheet, he dove. The water was mussed up and still he could see nothing; but standing on her settling deck and feeling something under one foot, he stooped. It was one of the bags of gold. He kicked it away. He felt around further till, his ear-drums and eyeballs ready to pop, he let himself shoot to the top of the water. He waited a while for breath, and then dove again, but could find nothing, and came up.

Now he climbed into the boat; and as he sat there, he thought what a pity it all was. The trusting primitive man, with just the little touch of guile, the dare-devil adventurer, the incorrigible law-breaker, but always the fine seaman—above all, the good shipmate with whom he had come to feel akin.

"Blast you! blast you, Chick Mangan!" he suddenly exploded, and then, the shells breaking all around, rowed ashore.

III

There was varied experience—the Russo-Japanese war for one kind—and four years had gone when Jack Gateley, the adventurer, returned to San Francisco. He looked up old Mrs. Mangan first of all, and found her, as usual, in the kitchen downstairs. Crooning to herself she was:

The Consuming Flame

"The cold north wind was on the Bay—
O, the Bay, the green-white Bay!
And o'er the waters and far away
His tall ship did sail that day.
O, the green-white stormy Bay!
When my lad's ship did sail away—
Over the waters and far away—
O, the day, the day, the day!"

"Grannie!"

"Oo-ra-lay!" exclaimed the old lady, and cried over him. And Jack almost cried too.

"And the Roosians—or the Japaneses—which was it?—didn't shoot you, Jackie? No? Well, they tried hard enough, I'll be bound. How many lost on that ship you were on?"

"Nine hundred, Grannie."

"And how many of you saved?"

"Three."

"Three? Glory be to ye three! But oh, the poor men, the poor men! But that's war, and we must take it like everything else, no doubt, we being what we are. But you're lookin' older, Jackie."

"I feel older—a lot older, Grannie. But"— he had to pull himself to speak of it—"what's this about that man Greig used to come around here?"

"Why, he's dead, boy."

"I know, but what about him?"

The Consuming Flame

"He saw Chick one day, him drivin' by behind a pair of those fast horses he owned so many of, and hunted the city high and low till he got somebody to make them acquainted. A fine, free-spending, handsome man, and lively—but terrible jealous, if anybody so much as looked at Chick. He wanted to marry Chick, and I don't know did she promise or not. I know she'd done most anything to get away, poor dear. 'Twas after you were reported lost with Lappen and the vessel in Asia, or wherever it was. She used to get so terribly tired, the poor child, of everything. And then came a sealer in to say that Lappen was lost but not you, and the pair of us, Chick and myself, talked so much about you that I believe the man got jealous. Anyway, the next thing I knew he used to be coming around here to see Chick and she wouldn't see him. There was something more than I knew in it. He said to me, 'Grannie, Chick's all right, but too straight-speaking for her own good—people don't understand her. I know I don't, and I've come to forty years of age.' He offered to leave her all his money if she'd marry him when he lay dying—his heart was weak—just take his name. But she wouldn't. So he left it to her anyway, and it's lyin' in the bank yet—she never touchin' one cent of it. Oh-h"— the old lady pushed her arms in a helpless gesture from her. "The poor girl's crazed, worn to the thickness of a straw. Wanted to die, she said once. 'What trouble's come into your life,' I said, 'that you want to die—you poor girl that's never known husband or child?' 'Maybe that's it,' she says."

Jack thrummed the table. "And who's this other man, Grannie, they say she's engaged to?"

"I don't know is she. Macron, a fine sort of man, a club man like. There used to be lots of talk about him in the papers."

"Why, he's most old enough to be her father, Grannie."

"True, boy. But who knows, perhaps bein' older, as Greig said, he understands her—which every one don't, maybe."

Jack meditated on Macron, a man of wealth and family, whose adventures in other days used to set the country gossiping. A wonderful man in his way, but——

"We"—Mrs. Mangan was running on—"we didn't hear till a week ago about your bein' saved from that terrible battle."

"Wasn't it in the papers?"

"'Twas in first—two years ago—that you were lost, and your picture. Chick was glad, and Macron too."

The Consuming Flame

"Macron?" exclaimed Jack. And abruptly, "Anybody upstairs, Grannie?"

"There is—Captain Prady. And go up, Jackie, like a good boy, and say a civil word to him. If you and him had some fallin' out, don't lay that agin him now, the poor man. He's that forlorn about Chick. What's there in the girl, anyway? Sure she's no prettier than was her mother."

"Or her grandmother—from what they say," Jack smiled.

"Oh-h—no deluderin', though I was no fright in my day. But that poor man, Prady, that gave up his steamer for a shore berth——"

"And why?"

"Why? It's not me can say, but he's hauntin' this old place since as far back as they say you and Lappen was lost. The poor man! go up and say a civil word to him, Jackie-boy."

So Jack went upstairs and said, "How are you?" to Prady, whereat the older man's face lit up immeasurably. They chatted of one thing and another; of everything but Chick.

Suddenly, unaccountably to Jack, Prady's eyes glowed. "I knew she'd be here, but I s'pose she's heard."

"Heard what?"

Prady only gazed incredulously at Jack, who presently heard the door open and close, and then

83

her step below stairs with Grannie. Then, by and by, her step ascending the stairs. She came in and shook hands with Prady. Jack, who was in the far corner, had also risen to greet her; but, seeming not to see him, she had taken a position by the window which looked out onto the garden of Jack's old home.

Jack saw how slender she was now; the old blazing color, too, had faded to ivory. Without warning she turned on him.

"Tell me about Lappen."

Jack told her briefly, laying stress only on Lappen's speech of her and his ending. "A brave man—and died on your account, I think."

"On my account, Jack?"

"On your account, yes."

"On my account," she repeated; then most irrelevantly, to Jack's way of thinking, "Why did he risk bringing you to disgrace, then?"

"Me into disgrace? Me? Was I of a child's age, or what? He loved you, dared for you, died for you, and you say that! God, but you've grown to be a terrible woman, Chick!"

"Perhaps so," she said slowly. And again, "Perhaps so," even more slowly. And then, sighing, "Well-ll—I don't imagine that all of us understand ourselves," and, sitting at the little organ, strayed from one piece to another. Jack came out of a reverie to find he was listening to the Lamentations. Jeremiah, viewing the ruins of Jerusalem, surely voiced a great sorrow; and the mediæval old monk who later set the prophet's lamentation to music, he, too, must have known what sorrow was.

Jack, sitting there, home after his years of peril and breathing it in, felt that it was much easier to die than to keep on living. If ever he went to battle again he hoped the ship's band would play what she was playing now. But no, no band could play it properly—it would need to be a church organ.

She ceased playing. A moment of silence and, softly, "Dan Lappen—off Saghalien—I hope he's resting well—and will forgive," and looking more directly at Jack, "You look more like the old Jackie now. But not so awfully sad, Jack. Come here—see." She was looking out onto the neglected garden.

"Do you remember the little girl, Jackie, who used to look across from her window mornings to you in your window, you a curly-haired boy in your night-gown, leaning out to point out to the Chinese servant what flowers to cut for your mommer's breakfast-table—do you ?"

There was a speaking beauty in her eyes, and Jack's heart was thumping terribly. He dared not speak, but only for Prady being there he would have gathered her to him. Pledged or no to Macron or any other man, it would not have mattered.

"And now it's a gambling house."

Abruptly an exclamation, almost like a cry wrung out of her, and she was off. The door closed below. Prady stepped into the other, the front room.

He returned soon. "She's gone—around the corner to Charlie Wing's—to the silk store. But there's a ladies' game there—such ladies!" He stepped over and looked gloomily out of the rear window. "That Charlie Wing, for all his polish and easy ways," he went on, "he's a desperate man. He is not used to having anybody cross him."

"No? But what's he got to do with her?"

Prady showed that he heard, but no answer came from him. Thirsting to hear of her smallest doings, Jack forced another question: "Does she go there often?"

"Twice before—this week. A silk store—but she never brings home any silk. You know," he went on hastily, "she may not be playing there, though if she did could you blame her? That Macron, I s'pose he bores her most to death—everything bores her these days, she that used to get so much fun out of the littlest thing." He looked up at the ceiling as if bored to death himself, and then all at once exploded with: "A wonder you wouldn't tell her to cut it out!"

"Me?" Jack wondered what had come over the man. "Me?"

"Yes, you." And after a while: "This Charlie Wing shot two men in Lima once—used to run a place in the Chinese quarter there. 'Twas me smuggled him aboard my steamer and brought him here—paid me five thousand dollars for it." He paused. "I wish now I hadn't. But I think I'll take a walk down the street. So long."

Out in the hall he stopped to look into the case where so many of Chick's old presents were hung up, those given her by the ship captains in the old days: shells, beads, bows and arrows, knives, guns, and so on—a regular little museum. Jack could hear the glass doors sliding, but paid no attention to that. Soon the street door closed behind him.

Jack stepped over to the rear window and looked out on that back area, and for no other reason than that she had been doing so a while ago. There was the yard to Charlie Wing's place. It had once been a fine garden, and a grand old mansion too, his father's, and he had lived there for a long time—had been born there. A thousand times he had played in that very garden, and so had she;

The Consuming Flame

and then he got to brooding over it, and over her
life, and over what Prady had said of this Charlie
Wing.

In the middle of his thoughts it came to him in
a flash. He had not believed that he could ever
again feel toward her as in the old days, but that
afternoon her personality had taken hold of him
again; and now he grew cold to think of her being
in Charlie Wing's place. In older days he would
have acted on the impulse, but of late he had got
into the way of thinking things out. So he was
brooding over it all—Charlie Wing, Prady, Greig,
Macron—wherein did it concern him?

The report of a pistol-shot brought him jumping
out of it. A dull sound it was, but he knew it for
a big-bored revolver shot. He picked out an open
window, a lace curtain across it. It must have
come from there. No longer puzzling reflection,
but down the backstairs in two strides across
Grannie's backyard in three more. The door to
Charlie Wing's he found bolted on the inside, but
the wall was easily scaled. He had not forgotten
the lay-out of his own old home—straight up the
backstairs he rushed and straight for that back-
room—he knew that room, too, of the open window.

Another shot, and almost at the same instant
the door swung open before him. It was Charlie

The Consuming Flame

Wing backing out. The revolver was still in his hand. Jack looked beyond Charlie and there he saw Chick, her head resting on a table as if she were weary—frightened he would say, if it were any other girl. On the floor was Prady, his legs stretched out before him and his back resting against the wall. Blood was on his white shirt front and a knife in his hand. Like coming death he looked. Charlie said something in Chinese and turned. A quick man, but not quite quick enough. Jack caught his lifted wrist, and the bullet went on by him—somewhere. He wrenched the wrist—he could feel the bones cracking under his grip and see Wing grow clear white with the agony. Before the weapon had hit the floor he had him by the throat, but Wing did not die by his hand. Over Wing's shoulder he saw Chick lift her head and he saw that she knew him. And he had no more time for Wing. He heaved him off and back on the floor he fell to Prady, who Jack had thought was all gone, but who now reached over and drove his knife deep into Wing's neck. The knife Jack knew for one from Chick's case, one of those ivory-handled knives from the East that Prady himself had brought home to her years before. And Jack had seen the mata- dors in Lima kill their bulls with just that same stroke—behind the shoulders and down through the heart. And so, no doubt, had Prady; and possibly, also, had Charlie Wing.

He took her up. Once she would have been quite a weight; but not now—the consuming fire had worn her. He could feel her lips to his ear. "Oh-h—but I'm so glad it's you that came to take me away."

Turning to the door, he said to Prady: "If anybody comes, let it be Charlie and you and me alone."

"All right," agreed Prady—"just you and me and Charlie. Didn't I tell you he was bad? He said something to Chick—I couldn't get the words, but Chick slapped his face. I heard the slap, and her voice like she was ready to cry; but not for fear, not Chick. 'Why, you yellow beast!' she said. 'Do you think because—' and then I, listening at the curtain, jumped in. But he had the gun all the time, he was that crazy about her—you didn't know that; I did—for years. He didn't give me a chance—seemed like he thought I was her man. If that wasn't a joke!" Prady laughed terribly. "I struck at him, but he was too quick—too quick. . . . So it'll be as you say, Gateley, no word of her . . . and I'll lie like a Chinaman—just me—and—and him—and he's gone—and I'm go-ing. . . ."

The Consuming Flame

IV

JACK carried her out through the old garden and into the boarding-house, meeting nobody on the way, to the same old sofa in the same old parlor. She was looking up at him as he laid her down. "I'm glad it's you, Jackie-dear," she said, and reached, weakly enough, for his hand. "I hurried back here to-day just hoping to catch you—I heard you were home again. I told Macron. He knows all about you and me, Jackie. Before ever I knew him long I told him. You said something about showing my colors once, Jackie, and I told him early. See here, dear."

She had been shot through the right breast, and the blood from the wound was spreading over her waist—a navy-blue serge, the color he liked so. Her throat seemed to be swelling and he opened her collar. No baby's throat was whiter or smoother. She put her hand to her waist and he unfastened it. She took his other hand while he was doing that and pressed it to her breast, then led it to a cord which, when he drew it out, he saw had fastened to it a medal. "See—your colors, Jackie." His own medal of honor it was. He had won it while an apprentice boy and had given it to her on his return home. He thought she had long ago lost it or thrown it away, or at least, in her heedless way, had given it to somebody.

"Macron never minded, Jack. That is half why I liked him, I think. No, Macron never minded. But Greig! I used to wear it inside; but this day I had it outside—under my coat—and he saw it. He guessed what it was and asked me, and I said yes. 'Then take it off and leave it off,' he said to me. 'I'll not take it off or leave it off,' I said. 'Take it off,' he said, 'or I'll go— and for good.' And I said 'Go!'" She looked at him then, a little proudly and yet timidly, as if he might not like her speaking of it. "He came back, but I never could like him again. Did I do right, Jackie?" The humility of her left him in speechless shame. He could have died at that moment, merely to reassure her.

"And there's a key—here." Jack drew it out. "Ask Grannie and she'll show you the box—it's got everything you ever sent me, every letter, every ebony elephant, every ivory pagoda, every souvenir spoon—every little thing and everything I ever saw in the papers about you—nothing else but you in it. And nobody's ever seen the inside of it but myself. There you'll find the letters— wrote but never sent—I want you to read them now. Read them . . . and you'll know I did love you, dear." She choked a little then, and he bent over to raise her up. "Sweetheart," she whispered—"nearer." To the impelling love and the beauty in her eyes he bent . . . still lower . . . and they kissed . . .

"It's the truest kiss I ever gave, Jackie. If it's a sin, then God help me!" Out of her weakness she rested a while, looking at him—saying no word but looking. . . . "I never meant harm to nobody, Jackie—to nobody—never, never! All I ever did I just couldn't help. Before I knew it was wrong, those captains used to pick me up and kiss me—and say things to me—like Prady. Poor Prady! I could burn for it now, but you must not think me better than I was—and I did. But I wasn't a bad girl—no more than that. I couldn't seem to help that, and surely they who used to know my father could mean no harm to me. But never after that day . . . that terrible day you left me. I never felt the same after that day. When you left me that day the blood left my heart. I used to cry the long nights through. And I hated the name of whoever might try to lead you astray. You wondered about Lappen—him, too, he promised me different."

She remained quiet for some little time. Her strength had been going from her. Jack feared she would speak no more, but she looked up to say, "And even to-day, Jackie, I got to thinking of when I was a little girl and you still a little boy, and I asked Charlie Wing to let me go to that room. It was upstairs in the gambling part, I know. But I went. And I raised the window to look out into the garden as you used to, but I saw you standing at the window there, and I drew back so you would not see me, and just then Charlie Wing came in and I drew farther back into the room so he wouldn't look out and see you. Something told me he did not like you. And there we were alone—and he misunderstood. Maybe I shouldn't have blamed him, for what could he guess of the heart of a girl, how after all the years the memory of even the little things will still cling. Maybe, too, good women don't go to the gambling part. And when he shot I didn't mind it much, only till you came in. 'He'll blame me again,' I thought; but when you looked at me as you did I could have died with joy. I wasn't afraid for you. I knew you would crush him if you wanted to. Remember the night you fought Prady? Every blow you struck that night I struck with you, and every blow he struck you, struck me. Poor Prady! Well, God forgive me if I'm to blame. . . . Sometimes I think my mother died too soon. . . .

The Consuming Flame

"And about Grannie, sweetheart. Be good to her, won't you? I know you will; but be double good to her for me. Oh, the nights she's laid awake while I cried myself to sleep, and she not knowing why. Be good to Grannie. . . ."

The blood was coming in little bubbles from her lips. Jack, wiping them away, tried not to let her know it. But she knew. "I think I ought to pray a little, Jackie, don't you? Won't you pray with me—and for me, sweetheart?—and for Captain Prady—and Captain Lappen—they were both brave men, weren't they, dear?"

So she began and he repeated: *"Our Father Who art in Heaven, hallowed be thy name.* . . . And now—yes, and for Charlie Wing too, for how could he guess? . . . Wait, wait, sweetheart—the baby prayer too. *Hail Holy Queen, Mother of Mercy, our life, our sweetness, and our hope. To thee do we cry, poor banished children of Eve, to thee do we send up our sighs, mourning and weeping in this valley of tears. Turn then, Most Gracious Advocate, thine eyes of mercy toward us, and after this our exile* . . . What's next, dear? Yes —oh yes . . . *That we may be made worthy of the promises of Christ* . . . *pray for us sinners now—and—*yes, *now and at the hour of—*of our *death-t-th—* What comes after death, Jackie?"

"Amen, sweetheart."

95

" . . . Ah-h, yes, A-men"—her fingers closing tightly over his. "Ah-h—ah-h"— the least little bit of a sigh. . . .

He buried his medal of honor with her. . . . He thought she would like it so. . . .

V

THE great battle fleet was about to sail from Hampton Roads. And Gateley came down to enlist. One thing sure, truth or no in the flying rumors—feast, fight, or frolic, whichever it would prove, here plainly was one of those who "hoped for the best."

Nothing happened to the fleet, but one day came target practice. Headed for the battle range was Gateley's ship with her men to battle stations. Down the line she was steaming, fourteen knots her speed, with all her port broadside and turret guns booming.

At their stations, stripped to their racing jerseys, eyes glowing, chests heaving, lips curving, but nerves under control, were the turret crew. So would they strip and look in battle, and no more eager to win in real battle than now. Round about were bags of powder piled up. Hardly prudent? No; but prudent people never make or save nations. The God of War there was

The Consuming Flame

the turret captain, Gateley—wide-shouldered, lean-waisted as a race-horse—astraddle of the entering hatch. Through his tight-fitting jersey his torso swelled; and his big arms, too, were bulging with restrained power.

Two miles she had gone, and nine thousand yards away a badly shot up target fluttered in the warm sea-air. Slugging down the battle line came the great ship again. It looked like a new world's record. From aloft they could see far out another solid rectangle of painted canvas being cut to flying ribbons. The time was almost up, the light of anticipation gleaming in their eyes—particularly the twelve-inch records would be badly broken. Boom, flame, and smoke it was along the whole ship's side, when pff! almost an explosion it was, and flame and smoke not reckoned with from beneath the after-turret entering hatch.

How that bag of powder was tossed out without an explosion nobody knew or could explain. The rules forbade speech till time was up, and another shot remained to be fired. And that was fired. "Something burning in the right hoist," said somebody then, and the turret captain dropped, almost threw himself, down through the four decks of the other ammunition hoist to the handling-room.

The Consuming Flame

Above him in one hoist the flames were roaring. Sparks of burning cloth began to fall on the steel deck of the handling-room, and there were bags of powder not yet stowed. "Don't touch that—nor don't wait for that—close your magazine doors!" he called, and they saw him jump for the sizzling little spark as they pulled-to the magazine doors, themselves inside.

Almost with the cushioned shock of the closing doors came the flash and a great pf-f-ff!—he had all but tossed the eighty-pound charge into the passageway when it had gone off. Two men came running in just in time to see him standing there with his arms crossed before his face. They saw him, too, smooth his eyelids with the tips of his fingers. "It must be terrible to be blind," he said. His jersey was burnt off his body.

The miracle of his escape overcame them. "You still alive, Gate?"

"I guess so."

"It's sure your lucky day."

"Right again, son—my lucky day," and went up on deck. The surgeon wished to have him brought below to the hospital, but Gateley begged off. "If you don't mind, sir, I'll stay up here," he said. So they allowed him to stay on deck, where he walked the quarter, from his turret to the ship's side, with never a word to anybody and nobody a word to him. Shipmates came up to him, with a mind to say something; but, meeting him face to face, they turned away without saying it.

And so he walked the deck—one hour, two hours, three hours, all that afternoon—turning sometimes to look out over the sea, at the sky, across to the other ships of the fleet; but no sign of what might be going on within, only when he would lift his head to gulp down the cool air. This terrible self-repression was too much for some of his shipmates—they went away to cry. But never a sign of weakness in him till suddenly he turned and looked up to the flag.

"Good-by, old ship—good ship, too." His voice was low. "Good-by, old Navy. I only wish 'twas on the real battle line," and saluted then the flag. Turning, he found a ring of his shipmates enclosing him. "Good-by, fellows," and—this in a voice low but clear as the ship's own bell—"Coming!" he called out, and fell full-length backward on the deck.

The surgeon knelt above his body. "Though hardly any need," he observed. "He was fated from the first. He inhaled the flame, and it burnt him out inside."

GREE GREE BUSH

Gree Gree Bush

QUEER how a man knocking around the world gets here a hint, there a hint, of a thing that has been puzzling him for years, and at last, all of a sudden usually, finds he has all the missing threads straight and untangled in his palm. I have in mind the case of Bowles. Bowles wasn't his right name at all, but we'll call him that, for it was under that name he enlisted in the navy, where they still speak of him as the "Gree Gree Man." But that enlistment occurred later.

Bowles came of a family up our way that, well, the newspaper men—I had a brother a newspaper man—used often to sit down and wonder if the Bowleses really did believe themselves so much better than ordinary people, or were they just trying to fool themselves, too. There is probably not much going on in a city that a dozen good police reporters don't pretty near get to the bottom of—if they're really interested. Bowles's people were great hypocrites and Bowles, being brought up to believe that he was better stuff than other fellows, naturally broke when the strain came.

Gree Gree Bush

Before he was out of college he had done a dozen things that another boy would have been put away for. But one day he just had to jump out, and in a hurry; and cut off from leaving the city by train or steamer, he sailed on a bark that was bound for the West Coast of Africa, on one of a line of old hookers that used to sail more or less regularly for the West Coast, going out with a small holdful—rum, striped calico, brass wire, and so on, missionaries sometimes—and coming back with a big holdful of ivory, palm-oil, pepper, and things like that. A nice, quiet business that used to pay about a thousand per cent one time. Perhaps it does yet. And it was a great relief to all the Bowleses when young Bowles got away without getting caught, and they didn't care how long he stayed away.

What I am about to say now of Bowles's doings on the West Coast is the summing up of what I learned at different times from a dozen people—a couple of ship captains, a bosun's mate in the navy, a dozen sailormen, stokers, and so on, who happened to be on the West Coast when Bowles was there. Out there Bowles fell in with old Chief Thomson, who used to run things pretty much to suit himself over a country larger than many a European nation controlled.

Thomson was a name the white traders gave

him. It may have been that Bowles—though Kipp was the name he took out there—possibly Bowles, coming of a hard-fibred trading ancestry, showed the old fellow a few new commercial tricks. He must have been of some material use, for old chief was too shrewd and Bowles too cold-blooded for anybody to suspect it was a matter of sentiment. So fat and wide that he had to swing his legs sideways like a duck when he walked—that was old chief but respected by all the white people, even though he was as complete an old villain as ever lived in some ways, for he had force, and he was a man who meant well by his own people; that is, after he'd had his fill of eating, drinking, and general pleasuring.

Old chief was at the head of half a dozen secret societies—at least half a dozen. Africa is rotten with secret societies, worse than any white country. Among white peoples, of course, those who want political office or a good grocery trade —that kind are the great "joiners"; but down there it was the ceremonies that attracted them as much as anything. In places there they still practise some of the things they used to do ages ago. It is hard to make people believe this, although in our own country the negroes still practise voodooism, and in Jamaica and Hayti they still practise Obeaism. One society, however, old Chief Thomson made little secret of—Africa for the Africans was what it meant.

And by an African he meant a black, and by a black, anybody with one drop of black blood. "One drop of negro blood always a negro," he used to say, or as near to it as he could in English. "The white people made that law—let it stand."

There are plenty like Thomson who want their people to rule everybody in Africa—blacks, whites, and yellows. Why not, he used to say, when Japan was planning to do the same thing in Asia, and the whites had been doing it in Europe and America. Old Chief Thomson carried his hope of this last society so far that he had had his eldest son educated in England, so that he might be better fitted to carry on the great work for the race.

There was a sort of branch of the society that old chief would not talk so freely about; but the scheme, so 'twas said, was to take boys and girls, especially girls, when they were young, and train them, so that by and by they would be able to train the coming race, to lead them to better things. The girls brought up like that used to be hid in the jungle, where if any man was found, he was put to death. Of this society old chief was believed to be Zoah, which meant Grand Knight, Grand Master, Exalted Ruler, Great Mogul, whatever anybody wants to call it, and clear on up to the 133d degree.

Of course, though talky negroes sometimes gave out hints, all this was mostly guesswork with the whites. There never was one who really knew anything about them—unless it was this same Bowles. And that was one thing they all had against Bowles—he was making up with the blacks against his own; and later, when he got tangled up and they got after him, in the Berg mystery, it was as much because of his being on the side of the natives as for the belief that he had a hand in Berg's death. This Berg was a steamer captain running up and down the West Coast, an American, a fine sort according to the rating of his kind, and he had married, many years before this, a girl who, it was whispered, had negro blood in her. Traders' lies!

However, this day he went up the river to meet old chief, taking his daughter with him. The mother being dead, she lived on the steamer with her father. Captain Berg intended only to run up to the lagoon and back; but he was a great gambler and he wound up by joining in a little game with Bowles and young Chief Thomson, who was now back from England. The game stretched out, ran into the evening—how late no real matter, though Captain Berg left at nine o'clock, according to young Chief Thomson and Bowles. Next morning, Captain Berg's body was found by his crew floating in the lagoon. It was known he could not swim, and as Thomson and Bowles said he had been drinking during the game, it was not hard to believe that he had fallen into the lagoon while looking for his landing.

But his daughter? She had gone with her father, Bowles and young chief said, and of course she must have drowned with him. Well, they waited for her body to come up. But it didn't come, whereupon people began to talk. They could not reach young chief, old chief had too much power for that, but Bowles had to get out. Old chief and young chief together could not save him. If he had not gone, some of Captain Berg's crew—he had two or three desperate ones among them—would surely have killed him. So he hurried away, this time to Manila, where he enlisted in the navy.

And here is what I started to say in the beginning: it is odd how we get onto a man's trail and lose it, then pick it up again, and at last see him run down. Our ship was lying into Rio Janeiro. The bosun was overseeing the unshipping of the ship's wash line. His great friend, Mr. Glavin, and myself were watching him. Quite a man, too, the bosun. Only the day before a big coal-passer had suddenly given a wild yell and leaped over the side. The bosun, without yelling, had gone over after him. It was a fine thing really, but not as the bosun explained it.

"The ridiculousest thing you ever saw," says he. "The big brute, he weighed one hundred and ninety and I don't s'pose I weigh over one hundred and twenty-five, and he couldn't swim, and tried to throw his arms around my neck. And instead gave me a black eye—look," and the bosun showed the eye. "But I give him a knee in his stomach under water, and a wallop in the nose out o' water, and when he let go, another wallop in the jaw. 'You big loafer,' I says, 'what you tryin' to do, hah—drown me?' Then I towed him to the gangway."

Here the bosun paused and reflected: "I ain't got the tonnage, though, to be pulling these big cart-horses out o' the water regularly. The next one 'll be liable to drown if he waits for me. Now if 'twas Glavin"—he pointed a finger to the chief machinist, who was leaning over the rail and gazing abstractedly toward the city—"if it was Glavin now, he'd 've just gone on treadin' water and tossed him onto the armor-belt shelf all in one motion"—which was the most exaggerated praise, of course, but going to show that physically, at least, Glavin rated high in that ship.

Gree Gree Bush

As I took to sizing up Glavin, a young apprentice lad approached him. The boy said something in a low tone. Glavin regarded him in mingled grief and surprise. "And only yesterday afternoon the master-at-arms tells me he saw you shooting crap atop of one of the cold boilers," he said.

"That's why, sir," said the lad. "They cleaned me out."

"Now look here," said Glavin, and gave him a fine dressing down, after which he handed a five-dollar bill to the boy.

The bosun roared aloud. "Some easy—you! On the level, Glavin, did ever you refuse a man a dollar in your life?"

"Yes, I did—once," answered Glavin. Only that then, but later he told the whole story. And here it is as he told it, the story of the Gree Gree Man.

I

I was a chief water-tender at this time on one of the heavy-armored cruisers of the Asiatic squadron, and there was an ordinary seaman who was also a great tailor, and being willing to work early and late, he used to make, oh, maybe, two hundred dollars a month over and above his pay. And being the best-hearted fellow in the world, he generally gave it away again. Didn't matter who

it was that asked Tailor Haley for money; he got
it, if Haley had it. And, of course, Haley never
saved a cent in spite of all he used to make.

Well, we were laying into Nagasaki one day
when Haley broke his liberty and came aboard
good and drunk. It happened to be right after
some American bluejackets had taken charge of
a souvenir store where they'd been paying seven-
teen prices for things and then not getting the real
article, though not for anything like that did our
fellows begin the trouble. It was that some of
them 'd made the Chinese cruise before and so
happened to know the money there, and when this
yellow chap tried to short-change them it was
like sounding general quarters. There must have
been, oh, a dozen or fifteen shop people went out
of commission before our people sounded off that
day. Well, our ship's party was known to 've been
around about there at the time, and the Japanese merchant who'd lost some money and come
aboard, he picked out Tailor Haley as the man that
started the trouble in his place, and a Japanese
policeman backed him up.

How did he know? Why, by Tailor's hat-
band, he said. He couldn't read a word of our
print, mind you, nor could the policeman; but
they both could read the name on the hat band.
Well, all right.

Gree Gree Bush

Now Tailor knew, as we found out later, that it was a chief petty officer who'd come so near to putting this particular merchant out of commission, and Tailor knew, too, that that same chief water-tender was drunk when he did it, so drunk that he didn't remember about it when he came to. Somebody had to go to the brig for it, and Tailor, with never a word, went; that is, no word except to say, to whiten a little the black mark against the service, "I was too drunk at the time to know what I was doing." As to the money part, everybody who knew Tailor laughed at that the same as Tailor did. "Lord," says Tailor, "you can put me down for most anything foolish, but when it comes to *stealin'!*"

However, after a summary court-martial, he was dishonorably discharged, but the stealing charge not proved. The officers, knowing Tailor, wouldn't stand for that.

Now, I knew that Tailor didn't do it. How? Well, Tailor and myself were great chums, and the afternoon this thing happened we were in a tea-house with the Geisha girls dancing and we sitting cross-legged on the mats, drinking tea while we watched 'em.

Now, casting back to make out why Tailor stood for what he did, I remembered—and there were but few men for'ard who didn't remember—

that day before we left San Francisco and the two sisters of this chief water-tender who came aboard to bid him good-by. And this chief water-tender, in spite of what had happened to Tailor, was a good fellow. And if he hadn't been we'd have overlooked it for the sake of his sisters; there was nothing promenading the quarter, let alone the for'ard deck, to be rated with them that day.

They certainly made prizes of the whole chief water-tender mess. They had everything going to do it—looks and figure and the quick wit, and the heart that's more than all. And so maybe you'll understand—Tailor worshipping on the edge of the crowd and that chief water-tender, the brother of these girls, hoping to go up for his warrant before long. Do you see what it meant to the chief water-tender and the kind of chap Tailor was—in his fourth enlistment and still an ordinary seaman. To Tailor the navy was only another place to pass the time in, while to this chief water-tender, brother of those girls, it meant his whole life.

Well, Tailor was dishonorably discharged, and there he was broke and blue, and ten thousand miles from home. So I beat the decks with a paper, one mess after the other, and they gave like sailors and bluejackets: chief petty officers five dollars, first-class men four dollars, second-

class three, and so on down to the young apprentice boys, who gave a dollar each; and many
would have given more, a month's pay some of
them, if they'd been allowed. Everybody gave
but one fellow—well, I won't disgrace any branch
of the service by saying what division he was in;
but this fellow—Bowles, as you can guess—instead
of money gives me a lecture. Said Tailor shouldn't
get anything from anybody. Deserved no pity—
ought to have saved for a rainy day. "The sun
don't shine every day," I remember him saying.

"A shipmate of yours as well as everybody
else's here, and a good shipmate, and now he's
down and out—what d'y' say?" I says, to give
him one last chance. But nothing came of my
pleading, and I said, "Well, the best thing I'll
wish for *you* is that you'll never have to ask *me*
for a dollar."

Well, after Tailor was put ashore, three or four
of us, friends of Tailor's, made up our minds
that the first chance Bowles would give us we'd
throw him. We'd already come to believe that
'twas him looted the Jap's cash-box, and not in
drink when he did it, either. No, he wasn't that
kind, nor was he the kind would do things out of
sheer devilment because he couldn't hold himself
in. So we rigged up a game one day to make the
master-at-arms open up his diddy-box, and, sure

enough, there was more gold than ever he drew from the paymaster. Well, that was no proof, one gold piece being pretty much like another; but only one thing did all of us here believe. And to think of him putting the Jap merchant and the policeman up to saying 'twas Tailor did that job! There was so much feeling against Bowles that all hands took to watching him night and day. Never mind at what. There are some things not pleasant to talk about—and at last he was put on the beach.

We all thought we'd seen the last of him then. But one day on our way home, in Callao a year or so later, we had a big international race—English, French, German, Italian, a dozen crews—I was stroke of our ship's crew. A good hard race, and forty thousand dollars comin' to us when we crossed the line. And all I could raise I bet on that race, and when I went ashore it was with twelve hundred dollars in my clothes. Of course it wouldn't do to take that bundle of money back to the States, so I was setting out to burn it, with a couple of good lads in my own division to help hold a match to it now and then.

And walking up from the jetty, that stone jetty with the big clock on the sort of a light-house, who should we meet but Bowles. There was every mark that he had gone to pieces. I saw him,

but didn't let on to know him. But he signalled
and I stopped. Maybe he thought I'd speak first,
but I didn't. I only looked him over. Did you
ever do that to a man down and out? He must
be a bad one to do that to, mustn't he? Well,
this was a bad one—I haven't hinted at the half
about him. And his eyes were a hunted dog's eyes,
his lips like a child's that expects to be struck
down. "Glavin"—he starts.

"You mean Mr. Glavin, don't you?" I says.

"It was plain Glavin once," he says, "or maybe you've got your warrant by this?"

On my word, I didn't think he had so much
spunk in him. "No," I says, "I haven't got my
warrant, and it's still plain Glavin—to shipmates
and friends."

He eyes me cornerwise. "Mr. Glavin, you
haven't the price of a meal, have you?"

"I have," I says, "of a meal or a drink, and a
good many of them!"

He looked at me again as if he thought I'd
speak first, but I didn't, and the shame of it never
stopped him. "Well, let me have it, will you?"

"Will I?" I says, and I looked him over again.
But he did have the mean eyes! And he had the
body that couldn't possibly hold the heart or soul
of any kind of a man. How a recruiting officer
ever passed him, I don't know.

Gree Gree Bush

"Will I?" I says, and I pulled out my roll with it. It made a bundle as big as my forearm, nothing short of a ten or twenty, except a few five and ten dollar gold pieces in my other pocket for change. "Do you remember Tailor Haley?" I goes on. He didn't say anything. "Well," I says, "before I give you a nickel you'll starve to-day, if it lays with me, for what you did to Tailor Haley."

He backs away from me, thought I was going to hit him, maybe; but I'd no more strike him than I would a leper with a broken back. "But I'll tell you what I *will* do," I goes on. "I'll go back aboard the ship and I'll tell them the whole story, and after that, I'll pass around a paper for you."

And I did, after I'd told the story to the new men who didn't know it. And I beat the decks, above and below, missing not a man, even going down into the bunkers below, and I came back, and not a cent had I. But as I was going over the side a machinist, third-class, hails me and says, "Hold up, Glavin. Him and me, we used to be in the same mess, and I remember now he passed me the butter once—here's a quarter to get the poor devil a meal." And another says, "Well, I never before refused a man money and I'd hate to have it on my ticket that I ever did refuse a man money. So here's a dime to get the hag's son a drink."

Over the side I went with the thirty-five cents and took it ashore, and giving it to him I says, "Here's what seven hundred men of your old ship have subscribed—thirty-five cents. It 'd been a thousand dollars if you'd done right. And that's for Tailor Haley," I goes on. "And if you meet anybody poorer than yourself before you strike a cantina or wherever it is you're going, I know you'll divide with him, you being that charitable kind." He'd turned away by then and was all but crying—in pity for himself, I s'pose.

"Remember your own favorite warning," I says. "'The sun don't shine every day?'" God forgive me, but the sun that day in Callao was like a glory in the sky!

II

WELL, I was home from the East on my furlough when I got word from Mr. Wilson saying that he was to be executive on one of the fast scout-ships and she was started for the West Coast, and would I go with him. A fine officer, Mr. Wilson—one of the best. After a man's been in a big cruiser and a battle-ship, a scout-ship don't look so great, but because of Mr. Wilson I shipped in her. Good officers mean more, after all, than big tonnage.

So we ran over, putting into a little place—I never knew the native name for it, but a little place on a point making out from a black river. And there was a little light-house on black and white painted stilts and a lot of black sludge around it. Before we went ashore, Mr. Wilson called me to his room.

"Glavin," he says, "I may need you on this thing we got to look into. There was an American ship-captain, Berg, and his daughter. He was drowned—or murdered—here, nearly two years now. The daughter was supposed to be drowned, too, but the relatives have heard rumors and they think she may be alive. They have an idea that one of these secret societies may 've got her. Now when we go ashore, you leave me and cruise for yourself till I'm ready to return to the ship. I can get all the official information I want, but the natives 'll never talk to an officer, you know. Off by yourself you may be able to learn something."

Mr. Wilson took the steam-launch and half a dozen of us of the crew ashore with him. But the man he wanted to find was at a settlement—inland—fifteen or twenty miles—so we steamed up this black river, dark even at noon-time with the trees hanging away over, and soft, squishy banks.

Gree Gree Bush

On the way up, Mr. Wilson spoke of a Mr. Thomson he had to meet, and I was wondering could he be old Chief Thomson, the same, they said, that Bowles 'd been mixed up with. I asked Mr. Wilson, but he said it couldn't be, as old Thomson was dead near a year.

From the river we steamed into a lagoon, and there Mr. Wilson met his Mr. Thomson, who was as black as one of the black gang's black bags aboard ship, though dressed like a white English swell—a long coat, top hat, and patent-leather shoes, and a cane, which he never forgot to swing. A big fellow when you got close to him, and could 've been a Congo chief straight out of the jungle, by his features, only he talked good English, with a topside accent. Mr. Wilson went off with Thomson to a sort of office building.

There was a lot of other niggers standing round, some of them not wearing much clothes, and while Mr. Wilson was gone off with Thomson, some of our crowd got to talking with them as well as we could—two or three of them knew some English. But we didn't get on very fast, and took to strolling round to see what the place looked like, how the people lived, and so on. And bearing in mind to learn a little something more, I got away from the village, nobody noticing me particularly, or so I thought, till I drifted up a narrow path that

soon led into the dark forest. After a time I saw
flying from a pole alongside the path a white cloth
with a queer black design on it. A circle it was,
outside of a man's hand holding what looked like
a war club. Then a nigger came running after
me and made a sign that I mustn't go that way.

"Leopard—lion—hippo—me no 'fraid," I said,
but he moved his hands faster than ever.

"No, no lion—girls—womans--Gree Gree
Bush!" he said. And I said, "Ho-ho!" and
waved him away again. "A fine time of day,"
I thought, "when I've got to run away from a
lot of women. Some chief's harem," I thought, a
little pleased at the notion of strange sights, and
pushed on. The nigger gave a sorrowful cry and
ran back.

I followed the path till I came to a stockade,
maybe ten feet high, made of thick trunks of what
must 've been palm-trees. The spaces in between
were plastered with mud or clay, and the sides
being so smooth I had some trouble in climbing up.

There were three buildings, long and low—
bungalows they would call them in the East—
and so much better built and so different from
any of the other buildings I'd seen since I landed,
most others being only one-story things of mud
and leaves, that I knew right away that they
must be for some unusual purpose. And while I

was puzzling over just what they might be, I heard women's voices from inside repeating something, like as if it might be a prayer, after some leader. And then came singing, and then like somebody preaching or reciting, and then they all came filing out from the building farthest away from where I was.

It was coming on late in the afternoon, and behind me was a lot of trees. All around, in fact, except at the one opening where the path was, the trees were solid; which was why they probably didn't see me, though I wasn't trying to hide myself. Not at first, I wasn't. I couldn't see any reason that it mattered at first, though soon, recollecting the nigger back on the path, I began to feel that this wasn't meant for me or any white man, or for any man to see.

They wore only long white robes with a red sash around their waists, and they were all barefooted and bare-armed and all black or brown —except one, who looked to be a white girl.

She was in the last row as they came up four by four, and I kept my eyes on her. I was hoping she'd look up. And she did. Just before she filed in the door of the building near my end she looked up, and her eyes—they doubled her loveliness! I don't know what made me—I never'd been given to speaking to strange women—"Look for me to-night," I called out, and whistled like a whippoorwill and slid down from the wall.

"Ah-h—to-night!" said a voice from behind me. I turned. There was a white man with a revolver aimed at me.

"Well, what do you want?" I said. It was almost dusk, mind. He jumped back, with a queer noise in his throat, which made me take a sharper look. "What!" It was—but I could hardly believe it—Bowles!

I jumps for him. He runs, but in four leaps I had him, and throwing my weight onto his back and slamming him to the ground, I took the revolver from him and turned his face up to what light was left. Sure enough it was the face I'd last seen that day on the dock in Callao.

I stuck the revolver in my jacket-pocket, stood up, and said, "Look here—you know how I love you, don't you?"

He didn't say anything to that. "Well, look here," I said again, and gripped him by the throat. "Now tell me what I want to know." I eased up on his throat. "Who are these women—these girls?"

"They're sacred. It's death if you're caught looking in on them—death even to be here. Only the Zoah and the council can visit here, and then they must all go together at some appointed time."

"Then what are you doing here?"

He didn't answer.

"And who's the Zoah?"

"Mr. Thomson."

"Mr. Thomson? The big fellow in the swell clothes? And he sent you after me?"

"Yes, when Daiko came back to tell him you were headed up this path."

"And what if I stay around here to-night —somebody'll kill me, huh? And that somebody'll be Mr. Thomson, huh—or somebody he'll appoint?"

He didn't answer. Perhaps he couldn't, for I had him gurgling under my fingers most of the time. "And I suppose you'll go back to the village if I let you?" I goes on. "And you're one of them now? And you got an establishment of your own by this time?"

He didn't say anything. I couldn't see his face very well—it was dark by then; but I felt I had it right. It was easy enough to imagine him, the kind he was, to settle down among them, with three or four oily, black, fat wives hanging around him. "And look here!" I gave his throat a fresh squeeze, till he must've thought I really intended to choke him to death. "Who's that girl?"

"What girl?"

Gree Gree Bush

"You know what girl. Tell me right or"—I think I'd have choked him where he stood if he hadn't answered. At last I got it out of him. She was Captain Berg's daughter. She had been kidnapped.

I was going to let him go, when I had an inspiration. "This Zoah, this Thomson—he wants to get hold of this girl, don't he?"

He admitted it. It was against all the laws of the bush society, but Thomson was planning to get her, nevertheless. He was even planning to kidnap her from this place—a sacrilegious thing.

After this I let go his throat. "You go back," I said, "and say nothing of me. If they ask you, say you couldn't find me, and they will think that I got lost in the jungle. A few more lies oughtn't to worry *your* conscience—and you'll be safe. If you hint of me—feel that?"—I gripped his throat again—"I'll kill you before the ship leaves port. Get that? You do, eh? Well, then, get out!" He backed away for half-a-dozen steps, then he hurried off in the darkness.

I climbed up on the stockade and for perhaps an hour I lay there, not moving or speaking. There were lights in the middle bungalow. After a time I whistled softly, three times together, the whippoorwill's call. I didn't know if there were any whippoorwills in that country, but I felt that she would recognize it when she heard. No answer, and I whistled again and again, softly. I was still whistling—I had heard nothing—when a voice below me said, "Sh-h——"

I could hardly make her out, even in her white robe, it was so dark. I made ready to drop down to her.

"No, no, no! You must not. They would kill you. But if you can come back—you are sailor and American, yes? My father was sailor and American, also." She spoke good English, but slowly, as though out of practice at it. "I have been praying, prayers of my dead mother, for some great, strong, white man to come and take me."

I almost leaped down—I don't know now why I didn't. "I'll get you out of here. I'll come back with a ship's company and we won't rest till——"

"No, no, no! that would not do. You must come only yourself—secretly—at night. I will show you the way."

I got no further. A series of calls rang out from inside. "I must go back. It is for prayers before bed. If I am not there, I shall be missed. But after—I shall come back. Wait for me, but oh, take care!"

As she fled away I did the foolish thing. Believing that if any others of the women there did hear me they would not understand, I called aloud, "I'll be waiting—don't fail!" and repeated the whippoorwill's call, and with that dropped off outside the wall.

"Waiting!" I fondly fancied her echoing it. But no voice of hers was that. A laugh followed it, and shuffling feet, and the stirring of underbrush, and heavy breathing.

"Who's there?" I called out—the foolishness of it; but I, aflame with the things I had in mind, felt strong enough to lick a whole tribe of black men.

I had my back to the stockade. "Who's there!" I called again. No answer—only the feeling that they were closing in on me. Bowles's revolver hung heavy in my inside pocket, and I drew it out, took a step forward—another, maybe another, and then it came. No terrible pain, but a dull blow, and then something like a great weight coming down upon me. I swayed, sagged slowly down, but came up. Again the dull blow and the weight, and "What a pity! what a pity!" I said to myself. And that's all I remember of that.

III

NEXT thing I remember I was lying in some kind of a low shack with a dim light in one corner and a negro fanning himself in another, and two negroes armed, each with a big, knobby war club and a heavy revolver—and no old-fashioned make, but as modern as any officer's service weapon—a queer combination, I thought, when I did think. I wasn't thinking too much. My head wasn't aching so terribly, though it did ache, but my mind wasn't clear and I was hungry.

I lay there, stupid enough, I guess, and it seemed to me that it was a dream and not real, when I heard a great beating of tomtoms. Before I could think of them at all the sound of them was ringing through me. Perhaps 'twas their noise woke me up. It came from somewhere outside, and, more than any thought of clubs and revolvers or sudden attack, it put dread into my soul. Slow, regular at first, but getting faster and faster, and that *yah-yah*, *yah-yah*, *yah-yah* which no white people can ever get, not till I found my heart beating to that note of it did I begin to feel the least worry.

A white man came in. It was Bowles, I saw— after a while. Then I closed my eyes again. He bent over me and put his eyes close to mine—I could feel him. He went out then, but soon returned with the nigger Daiko, who fed me a bowl of rice and a cup of some kind of kola-nut preparation.

Bowles watched me. "That's right, Daiko," he said, "feed him well. He must be brought to the sacrifice in his full strength. Soon now. Everything, the Zoah says, must be over by sunrise." I never let on I heard that, because I too well knew he meant it for me, not for the negro.

I needed that food, for I must 've lost quite a little blood. But with that food inside of me I felt better, a lot better.

The tomtoms stopped, and then another nigger came in and said something to Daiko, and he motioned to me as if to say that if I had done eating we would go. They led me then, with torch-bearers ahead and behind me, by way of a jungle path, oh, perhaps a quarter-mile to a building that was maybe sixty by forty, with an earth floor, high studded enough for two stories, and the whole side wall solid all the way up except for half a dozen slits up under the roof as if for ventilation. I'd been in half darkness so long that the place seemed bright to me, though it couldn't have been too bright, for there were only two lamps in the place, one at each end—big-bowled, old-fashioned, kerosene bracket lamps, like what they used in stables at home. They had reflectors behind the light and were set, oh, nine or ten feet above the floor.

The place was rigged up like a lodge-room of most any secret society in our country except that there was only one platform and pedestal, at the farther end from where they stood me. Thomson stood there. All around, the others stood along the two long sides of the room, close together. I didn't count them, but there must have been seventy or eighty of them. And they were all dressed alike, naked except for a loin cloth and some kind of wild animal's skin half covering them, beautiful lion and leopard skins—some one, some the other. Their bodies mostly were oily in the light. Every one carried a war club, one end resting on the ground, and a big re volver, like the two who'd been guarding back in the shack, and I couldn't help wondering why they carried the clubs when they could get such good, up-to-date weapons. But perhaps that was a regulation of the secret society, by way of re-minding them, the same as the tomtoms were.

They kept me standing there with nothing said or done for maybe ten minutes. Not one of them looked away from me, but I paid no atten-tion to them. It was Thomson I was measuring

up. And measured by inches, he was a proper
man. I couldn't help thinking what a grand
heavy-weight ring fighter he'd have made, and
wishing I could have a try at him before they
sewed me up, tied the weight, and slid me over
the side.

Bowles and Daiko had been sent out and now
they came back, the door being unbolted for them
after a queer knock three times given, and now
they let in Captain Berg's daughter. She was
dressed in white as when I had seen her, and
plainly the dread of something terrible was in her
eyes, but no trembling or drawing back. They
placed her face to me, and then Bowles and Daiko
were told to leave. Bowles, first turning to Thomson as if claiming some privilege, stepped close
to me, then slapped and then spat in my face three
times.

"That's for Tailor Haley," he said, "and that's
for the day you ran me off the ship, and that's
for that day in Callao. And the sun may be shining every day, but you'll never see it again."

If I'd only one arm, or just part of one arm
free, he'd have got his big discharge then and
there. But I only said, "You're a brave man—
you always were."

When the two were gone, Thomson came down
from his platform and placed a long, heavy knife in

her hand. For a long time she did not look up
at me. When she did it was to say, "Do you understand?"

I shook my head.

"You are to die. If I kill you I save my life.
If I don't, then I die and you are put to torture."

"Why not?" I said to her. "I've got to go,
anyway, and why not by you, and you save your
own life?"

"No, no!" she whispered and shook her head.
"Do you not see I am not of them? If I kill
you, do you not see how they will regard us?
You and I—we are of one blood. And there is,"
she was speaking in a low voice, "a way of escape
from the torture."

Her lips only framed the last three words, so
that nobody else there could possibly know what
she said. Her eyes sought mine, then she directed
them to the knife in her hand. "Save me from him,"
her lips said, though no sound came from them.

It took me a second or two to get her meaning. We looked at each other. "From him!" she
repeated with her lips, turning her eyes without
moving her head, and I knew she meant Thomson, who was standing rigid beside the pedestal.
On his kinky head fell the light of the big lamp
behind him. From behind me the light of the
other lamp shone on her.

Gree Gree Bush

I looked from her to Thomson and tried to guess what he was thinking of. I looked around at his councillors. To Thomson I looked again, and he smiled like a devil from hell; and yet there was anxiety in his eyes, too, while she stood there as if hesitating.

"You must decide—and quickly," came Thomson's voice suddenly, sharply. I think he meant by speaking in just that instant, in just that tone, to settle what he thought were her doubts.

With one last appeal in her eyes, she raised the knife and bent toward me as if to bury it into my breast. I raised my bound hands high as if to let her strike beneath them to my heart. Even as I did it, I could feel the thrill run around the room and above all the cry of pleasure from Thomson.

"Now you *must*," she said, and she had to reach up to make the stroke. One quick stroke and the bonds were cut and my hands free. "And here!" I said, and she slashed my ankle bonds—the whole thing in two seconds. With the knife in my hands I looked at Thomson and laughed. "Here," I said, and stepped toward her as if to strike; but what I intended was to pick her up and dash for the door.

Thomson called out and started forward. As he came, he swung his great war club and hurled it. I dodged, and as it struck the wall just behind me, I saw my chance. I picked it up, leaped into the air and smashed the lamp above me, then turned toward Thomson. He thought I meant it for him, and dropped on the floor, but it was over his head I threw it—at the other lamp.

And crash! From light to dark was quick as that. I swooped for her in the dark, took her in my left arm. "Now," I said, "here's where we'll have company going!" and leaped for the door. One man I felt in my way, and I drove the knife deep into him somewhere. Another, and him I knifed, too. I felt for the door—unbarred it. All was yelling and calling by now, but I knew it would take them a few seconds to guess what I had in mind. But the door would not open for me—it was barred on the outside, too.

"Stay here!" I whispered to her, and minding the two negroes just behind that I'd knifed, I reached back and drew them close, felt for their skin coverings, pulled them off and threw them over her. "Lay there till it's over," I said, and also pulled the two bodies—I made sure they were dead by a few more jabs—and curled them around in front and about her. At the same time I took the revolvers from their belts. They had no extra cartridges in the belts—none of 'em I remembered then had—only what they carried in the revolvers.

He thought I meant it for him, and dropped, but 'twas over
his head I threw it—at the other lamp

Gree Gree Bush

They were calling to each other now as if to get together, and somebody said something—Thomson's voice I thought—and I saw a little light, as if somebody had just struck a match. The light flared up. I aimed at the light before it could get blazing. A yell came, and at that I began shooting right and left. Whatever happened was the worse for them. There were seventy or eighty of them and only one of me. In no time all hands were shooting, while I lay on the ground next the bodies guarding the girl and let them shoot. Feeling another body fall near me, I reached over, and to make no mistake I drove my big knife into him—and drew him alongside. I reached around till I found the club of the last dead man and waited till the shooting was over which was soon enough. I piled this new body on top of the other two guarding her.

"You'll be safe now," I said.

"Stay here, you, too," she whispered.

"I won't go far," I said. "I won't have to," I added to myself, and stood up. There were groans and calls, cries of terror and pain, all over the place. And I almost laughed when I started out to think that no matter who I drove my knife into, it was an enemy. Every time one of them struck out, seventy or eighty in the beginning to my one, it was one of themselves that was struck.

Gree Gree Bush

All I had to do was not to let anybody grab me and hold me long enough to discover who I was.

And I waded in. And that big knife, fifteen inches long, double-edged and heavy—without half trying I could have reached the heart of a bullock with it. Every stroke wasn't a sure dead man, but pretty near it. Never a one I struck that didn't go down—if not dead, well on the way to it. And some of them yelled, and before I'd knifed half a dozen fresh ones, they were in a new panic, and I could hear all hands at it again, striking out with their war clubs. Then was my danger—that one of them would accidentally hit me.

So I took to the club business, too, but using two clubs, taking my second from the hands of the last man I'd knifed. With my left-hand club I felt for them, with my right-hand one I cracked their skulls. When I thought there was any danger to either side—I could tell by their terrible breathing—I'd drop low to make sure, and then let them have it. It was like cracking nuts with a hammer—as easy as that when you gauged the distance right. They couldn't tell me from one of themselves. Maybe five or six did feel my shirt instead of the smooth, oily bodies of themselves, but by then it was always too late.

When I felt a man give that most astonished grunt at close quarters, I took no chances but whipped out my knife and stabbed quick and hard. Three or four times I went down under somebody or other, but always then I reached up and slit a throat or a belly before a yell could come. That knife! A finger's weight on it and it cut through 'em like soft butter.

One time they quit yelling—Thomson's voice, I think, ordering; but I wasn't even sure of that, so crazy was I getting with all voices beginning to sound a good deal alike to me. I was beginning not to care where I fetched up—I only wanted to be swinging at them. But this time I stopped a second to listen. The voice must have been telling them how foolish they were to be killing each other. They stopped and I could hear them crowding together into the middle of the place. I guessed there were half of 'em left yet, and that wouldn't do; so I dove in among 'em and started swinging, and no mortal man, white, or yellow, or black could have stood there and been hammered and cracked by an invisible hand—like black Death itself—in that black place, and not struck back.

That's where I had 'em. And I went among 'em with new speed. Only when I felt the club touch would I stop, and only then for a part of a second to make sure, and then it was lean forward and duck low and let him have it. Not many I missed, and when I didn't miss they went down—and mostly for the count.

Of course, I got caught a few times. With bunches of 'em clinched in that dark I couldn't always dodge 'em. But when that happened and I went down under 'em, I used the knife back and up, and heaved 'em off me in a hurry. 'Twas like heaving the line off you in foot-ball, and I was a husky lad in those days. Of course I got cut and bruised, and what with the bruises and loss of blood I started with, I began to feel weak.

It had been a hot night outside. It was hotter than a fire-room in there. I could almost bite the air in chunks, what with the heat and the sweating and the blood and the hot breathing. Just the work of swinging a big war club the way I did for the Lord knows how long—fifteen or twenty minutes, maybe—that with the excitement was enough to keep a man up.

"A little more," I remember I kept saying to myself, "and it ought to be over." They rolled slippery around my feet. I fell half a dozen times quick, there were so many of 'em on the floor, and I was getting unsteady. At the last of it I let myself down on the floor and crawled among 'em. And 'twasn't till I felt there were no more of 'em left in the open that I began to wonder had I missed any in the corners.

Gree Gree Bush

My mind wasn't overclear at the beginning of it and surely not too clear toward the end. I think now that I was by this time half crazy. I felt and pounded in the corners, but no live one there. And then I stumbled onto the platform for the first time. There was one there. At first I thought he was dead like the others, but he moved under me. "Ah, but you're a cute one!" I said. I knew him. And what d' y' think I did? Dropped knife and club and went at him.

Half crazy? Sure I was. "I got you, Thomson," I says, and he said something, I don't remember to this day what it was. And do you know how I fixed him? Squeezed his big neck between my fingers. And I never let go till he fell from me, weakening—broke his neck, I guess, but I don't know. And don't care. I brushed him from me tired-like, to find myself breathing like a man just come through a quarter-mile run. And tired? Oh, terribly tired! And so I guessed I'd call it off, and went over by the door and reached my hand out for the girl. "Are you there?" I asked.

"Oh, to think that you're alive!" and she reached out her hand for mine. "Is it all over? And what you must have gone through! Oh, the blood—you're bleeding—everywhere! Oh, if the morning were only here so I could be of use to you!"

"It will soon be here," I said, and sure enough, by and by the rays of light came through the slits up near the roof. Then voices outside and a step at the door and the signal knock—three times repeated. I answered by the same knock I had heard them giving earlier in the night.

The bar outside was let down, the door turned, and in they came. It was Bowles and the nigger Daiko. I'd drawn the girl to myself to one side of the door, and when they came in they did not see us. It was so dark inside, too, and sunrise outside.

They blinked their eyes and looked and looked, for maybe half a minute, like people who thought they were dreaming. Daiko even rubbed his eyes as if to wake himself up. Then he turned and saw me, and seeing me he gave a shriek, fell on the floor face down, and lay there. Bowles stood stiff, so stiff that I went up to him and took his loaded revolver from him.

"Come, I said, "show me the way back to the lagoon." I turned to the girl. "Mr. Wilson will be waiting—no fear—with the launch and take us away."

I left Daiko where he was. I had no heart to hurt him. I had killed enough. Bowles walked ahead. I gave the revolver to the girl, while I carried a war club. "If anything happens to me, if anybody jumps out of the bushes on the way," I said, "you will have the revolver to defend yourself."

When we reached the lagoon the ship's launch was still waiting on the opposite bank. One of our fellows was standing by her—on watch, no doubt, for me. "Miss Berg," I said, "all's well at last."

"How are we to get across?" I asked Bowles, and he pointed to a dugout half hidden in the bushes. I made him push it through the black sludge to the water's edge. "And now if you will get in," I said to her. She reached one hand to me to be helped in. The hand with the revolver was lowered to her side, the side away from me. My mistake—to forget Bowles even for a second.

A cry from her and something like a dog's bark from Bowles, a report, and across the boat she fell. I leaped across her and the boat and whipped the club across his wrist, maybe broke it—I don't know—and as he dropped the revolver into the soft mud I grabbed him and held him there, kicking and struggling while I bent over her.

"Are you hurt, dear?" I asked.

Never an answer, and I called to her again. "Stand up, you!" I said to Bowles, and took him and set him on his feet. And he stood there

Gree Gree Bush

—as well as he could. And I brought the war club down—as if I was driving a stake. He went a foot deep into the mud. And his head was spread out like a red cauliflower.

THE VENTURE OF THE
"FLYING HIND"

The Venture of the "Flying Hind"

I WAS walking up Atlantic Avenue, in Boston, one day, thinking that perhaps I'd had enough of fishing for a while and wondering what I'd do next, when along came Glaves, and he slaps his thigh, and says: "Alec Corning—just the man. What d' y' say, Alec, to a little cruise down Newfoundland way?"

Now Glaves wasn't the man to go hunting you up out of pure love, and so I waited for more. Besides, when he said Newfoundland, I guessed what was at bottom. For that very morning I'd learned, too, that Annie Mann had gone back to visit her people; but Glaves, being what he was, I said nothing of that.

"There's a man named Cruse," goes on Glaves, "and he wants somebody that knows the Newfoundland coast; and he'll pay you well. What d' y' say? Maybe a bit of excitement for you before you see Boston again. And"—he added it almost without thinking—"Pinlock left for there a couple of days ago."

The Venture of the "Flying Hind"

That word of Pinlock settled it. Whatever the business it didn't matter now. Glaves could easily be a better man, but Pinlock! They did not make them any meaner than Pinlock. "Where will I find Cruse?" I asks.

So he brought me to Cruse, in the back room of a shipping office on Commercial Street, who sizes me up. "Well," he says, "you look like the man I want. And I hear there's not a harbor between Hatteras and the Straits of Belle Isle you can't take a vessel in or out of, fair or foul, night or day. What d' y' say, Mister Corning, to a yachting trip to Newfoundland?"

"Maybe," I says. "Though I don't know as I'd call it yachting."

"Well," he says, "if a man isn't yachting, what would bring him there?"

"Well," I says, "it's a good place, Newfoundland, for a fisherman to get baiting."

"All right," he says, "let's call it a fishing trip. But will you come? Glaves is all right in his way, but he needs somebody to stiffen him up like."

And so we left on the *Flying Hind*, a fishing vessel Cruse had got at a bargain that spring. I knew the *Hind* well—a fast craft, but weak built from her launching day, and six years of driving to market hadn't made her any stronger. Her

The Venture of the "Flying Hind"

frames sagged like the ribs of an old umbrella, and her spars buckled like a cabman's whip when we slapped the canvas to her in a breeze. But no matter—she could sail, and with Glaves for master and me one of the crew, we swung her off to the east'ard. The others of the crew were scrubs picked up along the water front, except an old dory-mate of mine, a young fellow named Gillis, careless as a drifting derelict in his ways, but game to his very shoestrings. Him I took to make sure there was one man would be standing by if anything happened.

We put into St. Pierre on our way, in the Mique-lon Islands off the Newfoundland coast, to wait for news and take a few cases of brandy for emergencies. From there we laid into a little place, Lowcliff, to the east'ard of St. Johns, where Annie Mann's people lived, and where was Pinlock's vessel, the *Polaris*, before us. Glaves couldn't wait till we were fair to anchor before he was on his way ashore to see Annie Mann. And Pinlock to the house before him.

We put in a week at this place, lying around daytimes and going to dances evenings, and I wondering when we would get down to business; but not worrying overmuch, for I was seeing Annie Mann every day. And neither did Gillis care. "Fine, buxom girls here in Lowcliff," Gillis used to say, and he'd dance all night with a younger sister of Annie's if she would but let him.

Till one afternoon Cruse came hurrying aboard. "The steamer from England's into St. Johns. Stand ready to put out any minute now." Next day a little packet dropped anchor near us, and that night we took four doryloads of Chinamen from her, forty in all, and the *Polaris* took three doryloads more. And we crowded 'em into the hold and battened the hatches on 'em. With the last Chinaman came Cruse. "Get out in a hurry now," says he.

It was a bit sudden, and I was glad enough to hear Glaves say: "Just another day here, just one."

"What for?" asks Cruse.

"Just one, just to-morrow, and to make sure I'll be back let Alec come along with me."

So we went ashore in the morning, up to Annie's father's house. She came to the door herself, and she was good to see—all smiles and curves and rosiness.

"Will you wait?" asks Glaves. "I've a message for Annie." Which didn't suit me quite, but I waited. After a while Annie herself called me inside. She and Glaves were standing together in the entry. "Is it true the *Hind* is going to sea to-night, Alec?" she asks.

I saw Gillis striving like a hero

The Venture of the "Flying Hind"

"So the owner says."

"And where bound?"

"He didn't say—if indeed he's sure where. But somewhere between Eastport and Norfolk I guess 'twill have to be."

She looked at me. "Is it smuggling out of St. Pierre?"

I had to laugh—at the thought of the Chinamen being mistaken for any St. Pierre packages. But before I could answer there came from the steps outside the scraping of a man's boots and a knock at the door. The three of us stepped into the front room, and Glaves was trembling. "Say you'll marry me, Annie," he says, "and we'll go off on the *Hind* together."

Annie's younger sister that Gillis was so sweet on came into the room then. "It's Captain Pinlock wants to see you, Annie."

"Tell him," says Annie, "he can't see me." That was a pleasant message to both Glaves and me. We heard the voice of Pinlock swearing at the door. "Tell her for me," he says, "that she'll be sorry for this, and Corning too, and whoever else is in there with them," and some more that was less polite.

More than the surprise was the thrill I felt at hearing my name coupled with Annie's. I had no notion that anybody but Glaves was thought to have a chance with Annie Mann. I was dumb, but Glaves was for jumping out the door. Coming to myself, I grabbed him. "A lovely bridegroom you'll look," I said, "with maybe your eyes blackened and your nose flattened." That by way of an excuse, for I doubted he was as good as Pinlock; also I did not want to see any brawling in front of Annie's door. So I went out the back door and overtook Pinlock on the dock, and I said a word or two and he said a word or two, and it being about that size of a place where there's no police to bother we had a great chance to try tacks.

Being as we were, of the one tonnage, with pretty much the same length and beam, as you might say, and the spars and quarters to carry sail, it ought to have been an even thing. But he couldn't maneuver—a bit slow to answer his helm, and maybe, too, I could bore into the wind closer than he could. Anyway, when for the last time he'd hauled his wind and his colors with it, I left him, he hailing the *Polaris* and I going back to the house. I hadn't been gone more than fifteen minutes altogether and Glaves was still talking. "Marry me, Annie, and I'll take you off on the *Hind* to-night," I heard through the door.

Annie heard my steps. "What happened?" she said.

"Nothing much," says I. "But I think he'll be putting out on the *Polaris* soon, and if there's going to be any wedding somebody 'll have to hurry."

"What makes you say that?" she asked. "There's going to be no wedding here. But to-night I'm leaving St. Johns on my father's vessel for Boston."

"And I will see you there, Annie?" says Glaves.

"Why, of course, and you too, Alec—that is, if you want to." She smiled at Glaves, but not at me, and I made up my mind I wouldn't call in a hurry.

II

IT was nine that night when we broke out our anchor. We should have gone early that day, the same as Pinlock, but Glaves had to go mooning around Lowcliff after Annie 'd gone off, having a drink here and a drink there. While we were waiting for him I, being handy with the brush, painted a new name under the vessel's stern, the *Zulieka*. I hauled a canvas over me while I was doing it—told the crew I was decorating things. For I'd begun to foresee the need of a change of name, and *Zulieka* was the most unlikely one I could think of. I had read it in a story somewhere.

The Venture of the "Flying Hind"

While Glaves lay drunk in his bunk I took the vessel out of Lowcliff Harbor. It was a pitch-black night, and only by the noise of a steamer's screw did we know that something was coming in. She bore no lights and passed us in a hurry. We had no lights up either.

"What's that?" asked Cruse.

"What could it be," I says, "coming from St. Johns way at ten o'clock at night, with her lights shrouded and at full speed?"

Only then did Cruse suspect it was the government cutter. "Pinlock's doing?" he asked.

I said yes, and was sorry I had not beat him up so that he would 've been thinking of going to a hospital 'stead of to sea that day. I forgot to say that we wouldn't have left the harbor that night only that I was afraid of this very thing, the cutter. Cruse had wanted to wait till morning, it looked so bad. 'Twas a gale of wind and getting worse, and the *Flying Hind*—the *Zulieka* now— a weak-built vessel, as I said, with her deck crawling under your feet. It was a hard beat out, but at last I shot her between the two lights of the narrow harbor entrance.

We made a wild night of it before morning. And three wilder days followed, so that we guessed there was some damage done along the coast that blow; and during it all, fearing stray cutters, I kept her well offshore. On the fourth day I swung her back toward the course of traffic, looking for a chance to run over Georges Shoals and so on to Narragansett Bay and Providence, which was one place Cruse had in mind to land his passengers. From Providence it would be an easy matter to get the Chinamen to Boston by train.

But that afternoon Gillis, on watch, made out a sail. We were pretty wary of everything; but I soon saw we hadn't any need to fear this, which was a wreck with only one mast left standing.

Glaves and Cruse were not over eager to stand down to her—Glaves especially. Whatever would the *Hind* do with more passengers? he asked, and what talk would they have after they got ashore? We'd all be ruined. Besides, somebody else would surely come along and pick them up, and so on; to which I answered that it wasn't yet on record where a fisherman passed by a wrecked vessel without trying to take her people off, and so now I was going to stand down to the vessel.

Drawing nearer, we could see she had been a small two-masted schooner, pretty well waterlogged now, a coaster by the look of her. While yet a mile away I could name her; but Glaves, though he'd seen her a score of times, and his eyes were as good as mine, had yet no suspicion, and so could not understand why I was so eager as we drew nearer to get alongside her. "She may be sinking under their feet," I says, and I *was* scared; but he had no suspicion till we were so close he could read her name.

It was Annie's father's vessel, and with him on the quarter Annie herself, wrapped in her father's great-coat and a sou'wester till she looked like any other of the crew at a distance. It was Glaves who bustled around and gave the orders then; but Gillis and me who manned the dory, and it was me who grasped her hand and first looked into her eyes again. "M-m—but I'm glad to see you again," she breathed, and that was enough; though later 'twas Glaves and Cruse who got all the thanks of her father, and right enough too, Cruse being the owner and Glaves hailing for the master of the *Hind*.

There was something of a sea and lifting fog that afternoon. Between the shifts of vapor we could see a steamer's smoke at times, but were not sure; and even if it was a steamer, I would not rush Annie into a dory till the sea moderated. It was one thing to put yourself or a fisherman like Gillis in a dory, but another to risk a woman's life in one. Not for two hours did I think it safe to take them off. And then it was in two dory-loads—Annie and her father the last to leave her.

The Venture of the "Flying Hind"

But between these two doryloads the steamer came down on us. She knew us without even trying to see the name, which I'd kept covered by a piece of canvas hung carelessly over her stern. She bore up and hailed—told us to stay where we were till morning, when she would take us in tow, or maybe send a boat aboard if it was moderate enough. And to prevent us from slipping away during the night we were to come to anchor and take in our topsails and keep our riding-light burning over our taffrail and another to our foremast-head; and to be careful to keep them burning bright, for if one of them disappeared for even a second they would take it as a signal of our attempt to escape and fire on us at once.

So there we lay, every one downcast and waiting for the morning, and it was me who caught it while Annie and her father were forward eating supper for lingering so long on the wreck of the coaster. I let them talk for a while, and then, looking at Glaves particularly, I said: "If I had to do it all over I'd do just the same, stay just as long on her, and so would you all—or be no men," and went on deck, where I watched the lights of the cutter, which was steaming back and forth like a patrol in the night. And watching her and thinking of what was next day before us gave me an idea, and I went into the hold, helped myself to two of the lanterns which were used to light up the Chinamen's quarters, and took them into the cabin, where now was Annie and her father, sitting on the lockers, she with her head on his shoulder, asleep.

"There's been more or less complaining of what's gone and past and what'll happen to us in the morning. Now it rests with ourselves whether we'll be here in the morning," I said, in a low voice so as not to waken Annie.

They couldn't see what I'd be at. Said Glaves: "What! you'd have the cutter fire at us and a woman aboard?" so loud that if Annie wasn't deep asleep she'd heard him, or so I was jealous enough to think. "Oh, belay that!" says I, and held up the two lanterns and lit them, and covered them each then with black oil-jackets. "Now," I said, "have a man stand by our light aloft and another by the lantern astern, while I'll row to the wreck and make these two lanterns fast on her, one to her stern and one to her mast-head, same as aboard here, but covered with these jackets till the time comes. And you watch the cutter's lights, and when the *Hind's* in line with the cutter and the coaster, then do you aboard here smash both lanterns at the same time, and I'll be on watch on the wreck and snap these oil-skins off the lanterns there, so the cutter won't

156

know but what they're the same all the time. And then we'll slip away nice and cozy."

Gillis wanted to come with me to the wreck, but I said no, and Glaves also said no. Said he'd need a good man like Gillis aboard the *Hind* to tend the light aloft. So I left the *Hind* alone in the dory and boarded the wreck, which lay then with her rails awash, as I could feel in climbing aboard. I mounted the shaky fore-rigging and tied the lantern to her masthead, making fast a length of halyard to the oil-skin cover and sliding down then to the deck, where I hung the other covered lantern over her stern. With the end of a line in each hand then I waited. A long wait it seemed, for the water on her deck aft was then to the top of my boots, and she settling lower with every roll.

The dory I had hauled up under her stern, ready to hand if she did go down, and by the feel of her I knew that she would go before a great while. Slowly the cutter's lights swung across the stars. My, but she came slow! But soon they would be in range. And now the stern light was in range—and now, Whsh-h-t! out went the *Hind's* lights. I whipped the oil-jackets away from my two lights. Below, aloft, they flashed brightly together, and into the dory I leaped and pulled madly for the *Hind*. In the blackness, of course, I couldn't see her, but I knew where she had been. Besides, the cutter's gliding lights were like a range to go by.

I rowed hard, but before I got to her I could hear her chain slipping. That meant I was not far from her. Then a voice, the voice of Annie: "You are sure Alec is aboard?" And Glaves's answer: "Sure of it—one of the men just told me he came in over the bow."

"So soon?" she exclaimed.

I guessed something then and drove the dory harder. I heard the jibing of muffled booms and knew she was coming around. She could not yet be under full way, but she was coming fast enough to make me hesitate. However, it was my only chance, and I laid the dory directly in what proved to be her course. Down came the lifted forefoot of her on the little dory. Down, down, I was borne under water; but I had a grip on her bobstay, and when she lifted I felt for the stops hanging from her bowsprit, and got them and hauled myself up. With every leap now she was increasing her speed, and by the time I was over her knight-heads, safe in her bow, she was sifting like a snake through the water.

I stayed up in the bow to get my breath, and as I waited I saw the mast-head light on the coaster begin to swing from side to side. While she was

yet swinging the taffrail light went out of sight—
p'ff, like that. Came a hail over the water then,
even as the lantern aloft began to swing yet more
widely. Another hail and almost immediately a
flash of flame as long as our foreboom. Almost
with the report the mast-head light dipped with a
rush into the sea. Another moment and a broadside lit up the blackness. The roar of it came
down the wind like thunder.

Crawling up, I almost stumbled over two figures
in the waist. "But is he aboard?" said the voice
of one—Cruse.

"Isn't he?" asked the other—Glaves.

"Don't you know?—he's hardly had time,"
said Cruse.

"No, he isn't, then," answered Glaves. "He
can lay around and the cutter 'll get him in the
morning."

"But suppose the cutter doesn't lay around—or
suppose it breezes up to-night?"

"Then to hell with him—we can't be laying
around here till we're caught."

I heard Annie's voice then, and crept farther
aft and stood by the house, not ten feet from her
and her father. "My poor vessel," said Captain
Mann.

"Yes, but your insurance is safe," answered
Glaves. He had moved aft, too.

The Venture of the "Flying Hind"

"It's more than insurance—fifteen good years I put in on her," said the old man. "And named for Annie's mother that's dead."

Just then Gillis came from somewhere forward. I could tell his step before he spoke. "You told me, Captain Glaves, that Alec was aboard and below; but I don't find him."

"What!" Annie's voice and the tone of it made my heart beat.

"He's in the cabin," answered Glaves.

"Oh-h—" said Annie. And after a pause: "But why isn't he up to see this? I'll call him," and went below. Glaves followed. Gillis jumped down after Glaves. I leaned over the house and looked down the cabin steps.

"And you said his dory was towing alongside, but it's not—nor on deck. There's but one dory on deck. Where is he?" Gillis stepped into the cabin light. "Alec Corning and me were dory-mates too long—look here, Glaves!"

What Gillis would have done I don't know—I dropped below and laid a hand on his arm, but looking at Annie at the time, and she looking at me. The fright left her face, and to see that made me so glad that I couldn't be mad even with Glaves.

"Maybe I'd better look to the vessel's course," I said after a little while. "Come, Archie, come on deck."

The Venture of the "Flying Hind"

III

I GAVE her all the sail we had, and all that night kept her going. By daylight we were many miles from where we'd left the cutter. But even so I drove her. It was a gale of wind and a milk-white sea, but still I drove her, and kept driving her till it got so bad below that the Chinamen came running on deck like rats. You could tell how much water was in her hold by measuring how high up their trousers, or whatever it is they wear for trousers, were wet. To their knees some of them.

And still I drove her, being in that mood, and I think I'd have driven her to some port or other in that breeze only she carried away her main-mast head. It was a gale of wind and a milk-white sea, as I said, and something had to go.

I had to take the main-sail off her then, and maybe with a young woman that two of us wanted for a wife aboard, she had sail enough without the main-sail in that breeze. And so long as we were stopping to put things to rights, I set the Chinamen to work, one gang with draw-buckets bailing out the hold and another gang to the pumps. One of them, who could speak a few words of English, just as much as said that it was pretty hard to have to pay two hundred and eighty dollars a head and work your passage too. I thought so too, but told him that if he didn't keep on bailing it soon wouldn't matter how much he'd paid for his passage. I didn't need to say any more. The English-talking one passed the word, and they all grabbed buckets and pump-brakes again.

It was gales, fog, and stiff winds for another two days, and we wondering where the *Polaris* and the cutter were all this time, when out of the fresh-coming easterly a sail came tearing. And soon we knew her for Pinlock's vessel, and behind her, just showing over the horizon, was the smoke of a steamer. It was plain it was a chase, which would make the steamer a government vessel. That meant it was no place for us, and so again I put the main-sail to the *Hind* and let her go straight before it.

The course of the *Polaris* when she first raised would 've carried her two or three miles to the east'ard of us; but now she swung off and came straight for us, so that by the time we had sail on the *Hind* the *Polaris* was perhaps a mile ahead and going at a great clip to the west'ard.

'Twas plenty wind, so much wind that I doubted our twisted mast-head could stand the strain of the main-sail; but it was not a case for doubting— I had to make sure. I knew that so long as noth- ing parted we could outsail the *Polaris*. And

I set the Chinamen to work, one gang bailing out—another gang to the pumps shortly we began to see that we had gained, and soon were closing in and before long would have had her safe. Only just then they slung a dory to the rail, put a couple of their Chinamen into it, and tossed it over. But hardly over—'twas a good sea on, I forgot to say—before it capsized.

Annie Mann, a proper Newfoundland girl, never one to mind rough weather, was on deck to see the excitement; but she hadn't counted on this kind of work. She screamed to see those poor fellows hanging to the bottom of that dory in that sea.

"Never mind," says Cruse—"the cutter 'll get 'em." And, turning to me: "Won't they, Alec?"

I doubted she could, even if she was on the spot—no rough-water sailormen their crews—and she was surely too far away. And in that sea they couldn't hang on very long.

'Twas a rain of tears on Annie's face; and when with that our English-speaking Chinaman pointed to the dory, then to one of our Chinamen, and said: "Brother," and every Chink of 'em looked at me, I began to wet my lips.

Annie went up to Glaves. "You're master of this vessel," she said—"couldn't you go close and throw them a line?"

"H-m—I don't seem to be the master for the last two or three days," he sneers. She looked to Cruse. "Well, at least you're the owner."

163

The Venture of the " Flying Hind "

"But not the owner of those Chinamen," answers Cruse. "Why should I give up my liberty for rivals of mine? They're Pinlock's passengers, not mine." From Cruse she turned to me, only to me she said no word. I couldn't bear her eyes. "All right," I said to her, but to myself: "It's jail for all hands," and, pushing Glaves from the wheel, I let her wear around. It was taking a long chance, but there was nothing else to do. And then what we all had feared happened. Away went our main-mast over the side.

"Now *we're* gone as well as the Chinks," said Cruse, and we all waited for the cutter to steam up and get us.

The Chinamen kept drifting away. They couldn't last much longer, that was certain, with every heave of the sea tossing them high. Annie broke down again. And I couldn't stand that either. "Archie," I says to Gillis, "help me heave the dory over."

"No, no," cries Annie, "I didn't mean that." But I pays no attention to her—it 'd gone past her now—only watches my chance to jump in.

"No, no, no," cries Annie again. "You can't get them—no dory can live out there. Don't make a worse tragedy of it." And she, being Newfoundland-born and a sailor's daughter, knew what a dory could and could not do. I pushed

her hands from my arm and leaps into the dory;
and who jumps in after me but Gillis, and I mind,
as we shoved the dory clear, saying to Gillis:
"You're certainly a damn fool, Archie."

"Maybe so," answers Gillis, "but I'm your
dory-mate too, Alec, and that means for rough
as well as fine weather. Maybe, too, Alec, she
won't forget me writing home to her young sister
for this," says Archie. And what more could I
say?

The capsized dory was up to wind'ard of us.
We worked up to wind'ard of her, and, getting
near, hove a line to them, making signs for one of
them to take hold and jump toward us, which one
did at last, and I hauled him under our stern,
Gillis, to the oars, watching the bad seas to keep
her head to them. A careless move on his part
and our dory would go over too. But a strong
lad, Gillis. He held her true, and I took a try
at my Chinaman, who was pretty well worn out
and weighed a ton, I thought, in his wet, woman-
like clothes. With one hand braced in the becket,
with the other I reached over and heaved high,
watching the sea to help, and in he came and lay
like a big fish in the bottom of the dory.

"A good job you did then, Archie. Now once
more," and tossed the line to the other lad. He
hesitated—hadn't the nerve of the first one. I

had to yell encouragement to him, and the Chinamen from the deck of our vessel began to call to
him, too. I did more than encourage him—I
threatened him as I again hove the line, which
this time he grabbed, but could not seem to trust
his life to. He sawed there while up and down the
seas were lifting him, one hand in the plug-strap
of his dory, the other in the bight of his life-line.
Again I yelled—every second of waiting was a
second of taking chances—and again came the
chorus of his countrymen from the *Hind's* deck.
So that finally he gathered himself and leaped,
and I hauled him under my dory's stern, and was
reaching down for him, had even got his hand,
when just then he let go the becket, which I had
also given him, and his weight came dead on me
just as I heard a great yell.

I could feel it coming, and braced. But I had
to hang onto my Chinaman, too, and the big sea
overbore me. When I came up I saw Gillis well
away from me, striving like a hero, one of his
oars broken and the dory filled to the gunnels.
But with his one oar astern he had yet a chance
to steer her to the vessel.

I was probably a hundred feet astern of the
vessel then, and drifting by. I figured that I had
hauled my last trawl. And probably I had, with
that almost dead Chinaman on my hands and the

cutter two miles away, when I noticed a broken spar—'twas our broken main-top, still attached to the big spar by the halyards and stays, but drifting well away from the vessel. It was no time for too much reflecting. I let go the hand of the almost lifeless Chinaman, and, grabbing his cue, kicked off my boots, threw myself on my back, and kicked out for the loose spar.

And made it, and was about to straddle it for a moment's clear breathing before hauling myself up on it, when the Chinaman, getting me in a despairing grip, pulled me back into the sea. The tide carried me away, my strength was gone —and I never so near the vessel. I said to myself: "Well, Alec, you're gone now, sure," and came up with only the hope of another look around to the vessel, to Annie, before I should go.

I heard my name called, and saw her, held on the taffrail by her old father and swinging a lead around her head—a strong, hearty girl she, but no Amazon. One, two, three times, and it came —almost hit me, but not quite—and, still hanging to my Chinaman by his cue, I was hauled alongside and aboard. Gillis was there before me—all gone; and I had to lie across the house before I could stand up.

However, we were all safe aboard, and the danger of it was forgot, when I saw the trembling

smile on Annie's lips and the look in her wet eyes
—it was not the salt spray alone that wet them.
And for the look in those eyes, had we been alone,
I'd have kissed her standing.

"You saved my life this day," I said.

"It's a man you are," she whispered, and to
have it said to me again in just that way I'd wish
the sea alive with capsized Chinamen, so I could
go out and get them all.

And the Chinaman whose brother we picked
up knelt down, and, with the brother, kept bump-
ing his head as well as he could to the tumbling
deck till Glaves picked 'em up by their cues—
"Yah-h—" and tossed them into the waist.
"You'd think it was a miracle happened!" he
sneered.

"And so it was," I said. "A miracle that a
girl ever threw a deep-sea lead that far."

IV

WELL, the cutter steamed up, but not to take
us then. "Well done!" says a chap with a mega-
phone. "But we'll have to take you into custody,
nevertheless. We'll come back for you when we
get the other fellow," and she tore on. She wasn't
the cutter we'd escaped from, but one of our own,
the *Sierra*.

The Venture of the "Flying Hind"

Away she went. And Cruse looked the saddest man you ever saw. But I couldn't see why. Perhaps nothing could look sad to me then, not with Annie standing by. I happened to think that with the mainsail falling over our stern they couldn't have seen our new name, that when she came back she'd be still hunting for the schooner *Flying Hind*. So with the crew and those Chinamen to help, I got to work, and if ever you saw Chinamen turn to it was those chaps. We'd give them the end of a line and motion them to haul, and they'd had things up by the roots if we didn't check 'em.

I had the wreckage of the main-mast cleared away and rigged the main-sail to the foremast, making a sloop of her, and once we got under way again we stood off to the no'the'ard, and next morning headed her to the west'ard. She made out pretty well. And with the Chinamen skylarking around deck when 'twas fine and ducking below when it was wet or we sighted a sail, it wasn't half-bad at all. Well-behaved, cooking their own rice, and clean as could be, those Chinamen. Only they did leave an awful smell of opium floating around below.

We crossed the Bay of Fundy by day, and coming into Massachusetts Bay at night with a good breeze stirring, we ought to 've been able to run somewhere between Boston and Gloucester before next daylight. Cruse thought Marblehead would be a good place, because from there he could get his Chinamen by trolley to Boston. So for there I headed her, and all would 've gone well, only the breeze died out and it was broad light when we drifted into Marblehead Harbor. And what was going on there but a yacht-race among a lot of dinky little jib and main-sail boats about as long as a banker's dory. No more freeboard than a two-inch plank, and sailing for the Emperor's Cup they were. And who was superintending operations but our cutter, the *Sierra*. A nice pocket we'd got into, but nothing to do but keep on, for Lord knows how many glasses were on us. Well, we drifted through 'em, a hundred or two of all kinds of yachts and excursion boats floating round to see the race; and with our busted gurry-kids—our deck 'd been swept clean in the storm— a few took notice of us, and to two or three we couldn't dodge I told a story of how it happened. It was more than we counted on, all that attention; but we had to keep on, and we came to anchor, industriously watching the race, with the Chinamen battened below, and all hands waiting for night-time.

Cruse went ashore during the day to arrange for getting the Chinamen to Boston, but nobody else would I allow to leave the ship. Annie I didn't dare let be seen on deck at all. But Glaves slipped me. He'd been glowering since the night of the escape from the wreck and ugly as a shark since the rescue of the Chinamen, and now when I was below for a minute's talk with Annie he hailed a shore-boat, and before I could get to him he was gone. "Well, maybe it was just as well. A good riddance," I thought.

But not so Annie. "Quick!" she said. "Send Archie after him to see what he's up to!" and Gillis jumped into the dory and rowed ashore. In two hours he was back. "Do you know what he did, the flat-faced skate!" burst out Gillis. "I trails him to a telephone place, and me not thinking overmuch of it let him talk. Till all at once it comes over me and I jumps in and hauls him out by the ear, but before I could stop him he'd got out: 'The boat you want, the *Flying Hind*, I say, is now in Marblehead Harbor,' like he was repeating something he'd already said once."

"A lucky thing," thinks I, "he wasn't aboard when I painted on that new name in Lowcliff Harbor. But go on, Archie—what then?"

"Well, I was mad enough, but I didn't let on how mad till I got him where nobody could interfere, out of town about a mile, and then I larruped him. When I left him he was there to stay for a while, and I'll bet he won't be telling any police, because look here"—and Gillis held up a bundle of newspapers—"I took these from him. Must 've been those gave him the telephoning notion."

When we opened up the newspapers we were surely amazed. There was a picture of the *Hind*, and the *Polaris*, and pictures of Glaves and Pinlock, and of the Newfoundland cutter we'd escaped from, and two of our revenue-cutters—all after us—and how Pinlock had sent word to St. Johns about us, and column after column of our leaving Newfoundland in the gale, and all about Pinlock putting into St. Pierre to escape the storm, and how he got drunk there and talked too much, and his having to hurry out, and the word passed along, and not a government vessel on the North Atlantic coast but what was on the watch for the pair of us.

"Whew!" I says, "and just when I was thinking our troubles were over," and goes up and hauls our staysail over the butt of the main-mast—it had been sawed off close to the deck. Then, praying for an early dark, we waited.

When the racing was over, who should come in and anchor handy to us but our government cutter! Nothing happened for a while, but by

172

and by I could see them getting up steam on her launch, which made me guess something. "Quick!" I calls out—"all hands tumble into a bunk and give a good imitation of men just off a forty-eight hours' watch! Let nobody talk but me. And you, Annie, you'll have to tuck away, too, in the lazaretto under the overhang."

They all got under cover in a hurry, and I made sure the Chinks were tight below, too, when alongside comes the cutter's little launch. An officer, a decent-looking chap—the same who'd mega-phoned to us after he'd passed on after the *Polaris*—rises out of her stern-sheets, and, though I didn't invite him, he comes aboard. Seeing him aboard, I couldn't but invite him into the cabin. But before going below he takes a look at our busted gurry-kids.

"Looks as if you been having a hard time."

"Yes," I says. "On our way to the fishing-grounds, but got caught off Cape Cod night before last, crew short-handed, and swept everything off except that one dory you see there."

"So I heard," he says. "Well, what brings me aboard is that the old man—our captain—is look-ing for information of a schooner-rigged fisherman we passed twenty miles east-south-east of Cape Cod three days ago. I guess you'd know her all right if you'd seen her—main-mast carried away."

The Venture of the "Flying Hind"

. "Three days ago," I repeats. "Let me see. Three days ago we weren't far from there. Don't dare go too far offshore in this old packet. But what about her?"

"Smuggling. But perhaps you haven't heard yet about these people trying to smuggle the Chinamen in?"

"Oh, them! Indeed I did. One of the yachts we passed in the harbor this morning hove us the papers that had all about it. What d' y' think? Think you'll get 'em?"

"I don't know." He strokes his chin and looks down at his feet. "But a while ago we got a message from Boston saying that that vessel, the *Flying Hind*, was now in this harbor. The party didn't say who told him, but somebody must 've been joking him in Boston, for I don't see any fishing *schooner* here. Or anything at all, for that matter, bearing the name *Flying Hind*."

"But you have to look around just the same, I s'pose?"

"That's it. Look around—and ask questions. And if"—he looked up at the skylight—"if I do see anything answering her description I'll have to do my duty, though I'm not over-crazy to get 'em. Why? Well, there were two of that smuggler's crew put off in a dory in a big wind and high sea —a spar-colored dory with red gunnels, same as that you've got on deck, I remember. And to put off and get those Chinamen as they did, 'twas a fine thing. And for that, more than any other reason, we passed him by and kept after the other chap. If I had my way, they'd get medals of honor, those two chaps that manned the dory, even if I had to send them to jail the next minute."

"Oh-h," I says, "probably a couple of fishermen, winter trawlers maybe, and it's pie for them to handle a dory in a little sea. But that's for one of them. What became of the other chap you were chasing?"

"Oh, we got him. Damn him, yes. Probably the papers 'll get hold of that soon. Kept after her till we crowded her ashore on Cape Cod. Her captain started to go through the surf in his dory, but a few well-placed one-pounders headed him back. Took them up to Boston yesterday. Be sure *he* 'll go to jail. A sight of difference between these two"—he looked at me again—"the chap that turned those Chinamen adrift and the chaps that picked them up. Maybe a lucky thing, too, for the *Flying Hind*, their stopping to pick the Chinamen up, but how they got far in their dismasted condition I don't see. And yet they *might* get away at that. Only I'm half hoping he don't drag in around here," he goes on; "because to-morrow the *Alleghany* will be taking our place, and she's got a commander who'd put his own father in jail if he broke the law." He was a decent-looking young fellow, as I said, and he looks casually at me then.

"Well, I s'pose he'd be right, too, the *Alleghany's* captain," I says; "and yet, I don't know, sometimes these fellows aren't the worst in the world. No telling what might be driving an honest man to make a cruise of that kind."

"H-m—what, for instance?" he asks.

"M-m—I could rig up a good story about that. Suppose now a fellow was in love with a girl and he wanted to keep an eye on a couple of other fellows who were courting the same girl, and neither of them much good?"

"But what's that got to do with— But hold up, there *was* a girl on the *Flying Hind*. But how did you know?"

"One of the papers had it."

"So? Well, we never told any reporter that."

"No? Then it must 've been a despatch from the Newfoundland cutter."

"M-m—maybe so. But what paper was it? Say, that's interesting, too! But let me see that paper!"

"Let me see," I said; but what I was seeing was Annie's eyes to the slit in the lazaretto slide. They were shining. "Let me see," said I. And, pretending to paw over the papers, "But maybe you'll have a drink while I'm looking them over?"

"M-m—I don't know but I will!"

From the locker in the state-room I hauls out a quart of that four-star brandy, draws the cork, and passes the bottle over to him. He looks curiously at the label. "That's funny now," he says. "In the *Polaris* we found two dozen cases of this stuff, under her cabin. I s'pose it's cheap in St. Pierre?"

"So I hear," I says. "Once in a while some of our fellows on their way home from a salt-fishing trip puts in there and brings along a case now and then, and maybe passes a spare bottle down the line same as this."

"So?" says the officer. "Well, here's your good health; and if ever you happen to run across those two men who put out in that dory I wish you'd give them my compliments, and say for me it was a fine bit of work. As I said, I'd tell 'em that if 'twas in open court and I giving evidence against them; and, of course, I'd have to give evidence against them if they're caught, for it's getting to be a bad business, this smuggling of Chinamen by way of Newfoundland. We stopped a lot of it by way of Puget Sound, on the Pacific, and now they're shipping 'em by way of the Continent and England—through the provinces and Newfoundland. There's a society, we've been told, that gets big money—a thousand dollars a head, it's said, for every Chinaman they can land in this country. And we got to stop it. And it seems too bad to see good men in that business, the kind of men that ought to be with the law instead of against it. But what's that?" He was sniffing the air like a game dog.

V

I WELL knew what it was, but being used to it, I'd forgotten all about it. And sitting with my chair against the bulkhead of the after-hold, I could almost hear them breathing hard against me; and I knew they had their eyes to any stray crack to get a peek at the officer in uniform, and to ease the strain, no doubt, one or two of them had to light up their little pills. I took quite a while to finish my drink, not even opening my eyes over the top of the glass till I'd got it right.

"It's the sulphur we burned trip before last," I said at last. "Once every year we fishermen seal up everything below and burn sulphur to fumigate her, to kill any stray rats and so on." Even as I spoke I could see Annie over his shoulder, her head and shoulders out of the lazaretto, and her scared eyes on mine. "Yes," I said, "it's the old sulphur still smelling. Takes two or three weeks to sea sometimes to clear it out."

"Oh, that's it?" he says. "I'm glad to hear that," and after another drink goes up on deck and into his launch. Only as he was about to step over the rail, taking another look around, he says: "Got her mast stepped pretty well forward, hasn't she, for a sloop rig?"

"She's one of those Zanzibar models," I says, quick, too quick; for I doubt if I could 've explained a Zanzibar model off hand.

"Zanzibar?" he repeats, relieved-like. "Well, that's a new one on me, but I'll bet you know all about them," and he smiled. He didn't say any more, only, as his launch went under our stern, he pointed out her name, *Zulieka*. "We couldn't find it in the register," he says.

"Naturally," I said, "seeing as she was named new since the last register was printed."

He looked me fair in the eyes then, and—'twas the first time—he laughed out loud. "You can explain it all over to the captain of the *Alleghany* to-morrow," he says, and, laughing again, waves his hand and steams off.

"Oh, yes," I said to myself, "I can see myself waiting for that revenue captain in the morning."

That night, after dark, Gillis and I rowed ashore those forty-two Chinamen, eleven to a time in the dory. There was a little chop on, and, with thirteen of us in the dory, they had to bail like blue devils with their little round hats to keep her from filling. And Cruse and his agents, who were waiting, took 'em to Boston on the trolleys, half a dozen to a time.

I put Annie Mann and her father ashore too. On leaving, she said: "Be careful and get away long before daylight, Alec. Let all the Glaveses and Pinlocks and Cruses be caught—it's in their business—but not you, Alec. Nor you either, Archie," stepping over to him. "No sister of mine must marry a law-breaker," and a few words more to me, and then a few from me that had maybe more of love than of law in them.

We worked our way out among the yachting fleet in the dark, and next day being drizzly, it was a good chance to run her into a safe place on the north side of Cape Ann. And there we let her lay a while. And the extra head-money on those two Chinamen we picked up in the dory was more than enough to pay for the broken main-mast and all the damage of the gale. And Cruse after a time sold her to a Portugee for a packet between New Bedford and the Azores Islands, though Cruse—only his name wasn't Cruse for a while— had to sacrifice all the profit of the trip in the sale. For fast as the devil though she was, which suited the Portuguese packet service, she was a bit loose in her planking.

What became of Glaves, I don't know; but he never darkened Annie Mann's door again. And Gillis and I—we were satisfied to go back fishing.

THE CRUISE O' THE
"BOUNDING BOY"

The Cruise o' the "Bounding Boy"

ON to the port wing-deck—on our ship the coziest nook from which to view things, and no whole ship's company to disturb—we strolled this afternoon to see what was doing; and who should be there before us but Cahalan, the same old untamable Cahalan, and the same old rating badge on his sleeve. Nobody in the deck division had been long enough in the service to remember when Cahalan didn't rate as a bosun's mate, first class.

When we were last shipmates with Cahalan he was a short-timer, and his daily chant had been, "No more navy for me after I'm paid off this time"; which, of course, coming from an old flatfoot, is never taken seriously. It is only your one and two service-stripers who don't come back. Even the officers; you can hear them sometimes, on their blue days down in the wardroom country, tell how they're going to resign—yes, sir, going to resign and raise chickens, by gad! or get a job

with some power company somewhere ashore.
And how many of them do? And why don't they?

And why hadn't Cahalan? Well, he had,
partly; at least he had stayed beyond his four
months' furlough. And that meant a lot—forfeit-
ing his continuous-service privileges. And why?
we wondered.

We were eager enough to hear what Cahalan
would have to say, but he seemed to be engrossed,
so gloomily engrossed, judging by his profile expression, with the ship's launch which, with a
cargo of young women, two or three of them quite
pretty, was just then steaming up to the ship's side,
that we did not break in on him; only when at
last he did turn around one of us said, "Hello,"
and he said, "Hello," and, further, "Look,"
meaning thereby for us to observe the young
ladies strategically disposed around the quarter-
deck. "Girls enough for all," commented Cahalan, "even for the middies almost. Look at 'em,
cruising outboard like a lot of little patrol boats
at a review, waiting to swoop down on anything
that drifts across the line!"

But we were not interesting ourselves in ward-
room or steerage procedure. "The last time we
saw you you were beating it up the dock, waving
your hand back at the ship and saying, 'Never
again for me.' What brought you back?"

"Would you believe it—Wimmen!" he exploded suddenly. "Yes, wimmen! And another man's judgment of 'em, mind you, not my own. But when a man's been a year to sea, same as this chap 'd been, what c'n you expect?"

"Or even when you haven't been any year to sea; when you're ashore the whole time?"

"No, no, no," protested Cahalan; "not so bad as that. When you get into port occasionally to kind o' keep the run o' their development you're not altogether out of it; but when"—and so on for an uninterrupted run of a half-hour or so before we could swing him back to the charted course. Cahalan was a great hand to fly off like that, and when he did fly off it was for no little flying-fish leaps, but long, steady, cloud-reaching flights.

"Well, when I was paid off in 'Frisco that day there were just two things I had in mind. One, I wasn't going back to the navy; and the other, I was going to see my good old mother, who lives in Brooklyn. And I had the best part of two years' back pay and a ticket to New York in my pocket, the ticket through Canada so that I could have a look at the country along the way. All right! But it was a hot day going through the valley and I hadn't had a drink in three months. You know how it is being a prohibitionist, whether you will or no, aboard ship. Maybe the tea-drinking old ladies think it's a grand scheme, but maybe, too, those old ladies don't know it all. Did they ever stop to think, d' y' s'pose, how a coal-passer feels who's been shovelling coal for four hours next a hot furnace and he comes up in the air, and he'd give his month's pay for a bottle of cold beer? But he can't have it, not if he'd give his life for it. No. But the old ladies who made the law can have their twelve or fifteen cups o' tea a day. I wonder would they put up a holler if you and me was to pass a law sayin' they couldn't?

"Well, I didn't start out to deliver any sermon. It was a hot day, and I got off at Seattle to get a drink. And you know how it is about a drink No man is goin' to stop at one bottle of beer after he's stayed away from it three months. Of course not. So I had another, and a third, and maybe a fourth or a fifth; and then I stopped to take soundings—and maybe make a new departure for a different, maybe a better label o' beer; for when you got plenty of money in your pocket you might's well have your choice, mightn't you? Sure.

"Well, I fetched up at a place called Tagen's, a sort of hotel with a barroom at one end and a caffy at the other, a place that seemed to be popular with foolish chaps back from the Klondike and other foolish chaps like myself just back from sea. There I happened to sit down at the same table with what looked like a seafarin' man. And so he turned out, a sealing captain named Patten and a pretty decent sort, too. And it wasn't hard to see he was at home in the place, for soon he introduced me to a soft-stepping chap he called Johnnie, who seemed to rate as a sort of master-at-arms and canteen yeoman, both; for when he wasn't around noticin' things he was makin' change.

" 'The boss?' I asked, after Johnnie'd had a drink with us—only he took a cigar instead, a quarter one, which he put in his pocket; goin' to smoke it later.

" 'No, no, there's the boss in the office,' says Patten; 'him reading the paper in his shirt-sleeves. He don't have anything to do but spend the money. He leaves everything to Johnnie.' Well, a few more drinks, and Patten was telling me his life's history, and I says to myself, 'You're not the worst in the world, only you sure oughtn't to be allowed to be cruisin' around here without a land compass and a corrected up-to-date shore-goin' chart.'

"Anyway, 'Come, Cahalan,' he says after a while, 'till I introduce you to the future Mrs. Patten,' and steers me up to the caffy at the other end of the hotel, where was a big blonde woman in the cashier's cage.

" 'Ain't she a queen?' says Patten, and taking a table where he could see her, orders enough for general mess; and all through the meal was making eyes at her, and when she wasn't making change she'd smile at him, too, but in a most proper way. 'A perfect lady,' says Patten, 'who won't brook no familiarity.'

" 'Yes,' says I, 'easy to see that. If you doubt the goods look at the label—no other brand——'

" 'Huh!' he says.

" 'Easy to see,' I hurries on to say, 'that she's sure a perfect lady.'

" 'They don't none of them get fresh with her,' explains Patten.

" 'Why should they? I mean, of course not, Cap. But ain't she a pretty good tonnage for a light-armored craft like you to be engagin'?' And then, so's not to hurt his feelin's, 'Ain't she kind of a little on the buxom model?'

" 'Oh!' says Patten, 'I likes 'em buxom.'

"Buxom she sure was. A battle-ship I'd call her, and couldn't help imaginin' her steamin' down a crowded street and bowling 'em to the right and left off each bow.

" 'Ain't she a queen, though, Addie?' goes on Patten. And now, what're you going to do with a man like that? Only ten days ashore, after a year at sea, and already sealing up his judgments. Let a man stay away long enough, 'specially if it's brown, yellow, and black he's been mixin' with, and almost any upstandin' white woman 'll get him. 'I'm goin' off to make a little pile and come back and marry her,' he goes on, 'and what d'y' say to shippin' with me as mate?'

" 'For a sealing trip?'

" 'For a sealing trip—or whatever it develops into.' He stops to give me a good look over, and I says, 'Better not tell me yet, for maybe I won't go.'

"When Patten went up to settle for the check there was some little goo-gooin' between himself and the cashier, which I couldn't help no·icin', no more than I could that she didn't have to r.·ℊ up any cash register, and, noticin' that, I remembered that, at the other end of the house, where the smooth bartender made the change, there wasn't any cash register either. I mentions this to Patten when we were outside.

"'Oh!' explains Patten, to that, 'Tagen trusts 'em both. And why shouldn't he? They make all his money for him. Why, Johnnie's got a thousand of my money—goin' to let me in on a minin' proposition. A great fellow, Johnnie. But how about that sealin' trip with me?'

The Cruise o' the "Bounding Boy"

" 'No,' I says, 'I'll pass that up now, Cap. My old mother, y'see, she lives in the middle of a three-deck house in Brooklyn, with ten Lithuanians topside and a family named Wyzinski on the deck below, and I'm goin' to see her and move her out of there.' And never did I mean anything like I meant that. But, once having dropped anchor, of course you've got to have a look at a port before you get under way again—of course. And a week later"—Cahalan spat reminiscently over the side—"with not enough in my pocket to buy a cup of coffee, I patrolled the water-front one mornin' till I met Patten, and, without askin' any questions, I signed on as mate of the *Bounding Boy*, a schooner with a deep forefoot, a mixed crew, and a ss-eyed, English-speaking Jap cook that was also cabin-boy, named Zippy.

" 'Now,' says Patten, 'here's my scheme. There's a fur company up thereaway that's been doin' a nice quiet business with the huskies in the Aleutians, collecting skins for 'em—otters, foxes, seals and one kind or another, fine rich skins that bring a big price in 'Frisco. And here's how they work it. Every now and then, when the huskies have a nice pile of skins collected, the fur company's vessel comes along, hoists the company's flag to the foretruck, the crew go ashore, take the skins, give the huskies a big official document—a fine big sheet of paper with a big blue ribbon and a splash of red wax—all official, you know—and sail off.'

" 'Well?' I says.

" 'Well,' he says, 'what's the matter with us sailin' up and collectin' some of them skins?'

" 'Sort of loot the Leuts!' I says to him.

"I s'pose bein' brought up in the navy makes a difference, but it looked to me like high piracy, and I said so.

" 'Sho!' says Patten. 'A bunch o' Roosians and Japs owns the company.'

"Well, I didn't figure out where they bein' Roosians and Japs let me out, but I was in for it, and so we gets a lot of fine, big, official-looking papers, blue ribbons, and red wax, and sails out. And wherever we saw a fat pile of skins we'd hoist the foreign fur company's flag to the fore, sail in, go ashore, say 'How!' to the huskies, open up a little keg, hand the red stuff around, get 'em all pie-eyed, collect the skins, give them a receipt —all official, blue ribbon and the red-wax seal— leave 'em to finish the little keg, and sail away.

"We were doin' a magnificent business, had the main-hold of the *Bounding Boy* pretty well filled up, and the same hadn't cost us more than, well, say, than twenty-one or two ten gallon kegs of about that class of rum which they used to hand

out to drunken sailors along the Barbary Coast
before the fire, and Patten was talking of 'Frisco,
Seattle, and the Queen of Tagen's bar, when one
day a Jap he did business with at one of the stations up there came out in a little sailboat to tell
him he'd better not go back to the States with the
skins, that the cutter was watching out for us; but
to take them to Vladivostok, where was a man—
Patten made a note of the name—a safe man who
bought skins for the Russian market and without
askin' too many questions.

"I didn't like the Jap's looks, but Patten reminded me that I didn't like Japs anyway, which
was true; and so we swung the *Boy* off for the
other shore of the Pacific, and not a thing happened during the whole passage till we came to
anchor in the harbor of Vladivostok, when a
Russian official took the vessel in charge and, casting the rest of the crew loose, threw Patten and
me into a little stone jail and held us there for
three weeks, which certainly surprised us some.

"Out in the light of the sun again, the first
news—from a whiskered, belted, good-natured
Russian, who could talk English—was that the
schooner had been auctioned off the day before
to pay the fine. 'What did she bring?' asks
Patten.

" 'Twenty-two hundred and fifty rubles.'

The Cruise o' the "Bounding Boy"

" 'What! My fine *Bounding Boy* that cost me six times that only fifteen months ago!' yells Patten. 'And how much was the fine?'

"And the Russian, not a smile out of him, says, ' Twenty-two hundred and fifty rubles.'

" 'Whee-yew!' and Patten has to sit down to fan himself.

" 'Not even a few loose copecks for a drink?' I asks. 'No? They surely made a proper job, didn't they? And how about the furs?' I asks.

" 'Oh, the head of the fur company, from which you stole them, came to Vladivostok—he was here truly before your ship—he took them.'

" 'And what'd he have to say?'

" 'Said that now, as he had his furs, he would not prosecute further. Very good of him.'

" 'Damn good,' I says. 'But who bought the schooner?'

" 'A Japanese gentleman. His name? Wait. But no, I do not recollect his name.'

"Well, we both knew too much of Russian officials to protest. The whole outfit, Russians and Japs, were in together, and they weren't letting the little matter of the late war interfere with business. Well, the schooner was gone, and I was only wishin' I had a smoke. But Patten breaks out with, 'And all my money stored under her cabin run!' and sits down on a doorstep, and

there I left him, to go back and put a few more
questions to that Russian who spoke such good
English; and he told me that the rest of the crew
had shipped on any old kind of a craft to get away
—all but the four Japs, who had gone off on the
schooner with the new owner.

" 'Zippy—a low-sized, cross-eyed chap—was he
one of them?' I asks him. 'Yes, he was one of
them,' and I hurries back to Patten. 'All those
chaps going off in the *Boy* means that she's bound
for Japan,' I says to Patten. 'Don't you remember they were all figurin' on how they'd get home
the whole cruise? And Zippy the cook's one
of them. And Zippy,' I went on, 'was the only
one who could come in and out of the cabin when
he pleased.' And at that Patten came to himself.

" 'Then if I want to see that money again I
got to find Zippy, and the easiest way to find
Zippy is to find the vessel, hah?' said Patten, and
offers me double wages for the whole cruise if I'd
go after the vessel with him. And, of course, I
went—'twas as short a way home as any other—
and, besides, I wanted to get a crack at our old
cook, too. So the pair of us shipped on a little
steamer bound for Hong-Kong and way ports.
Patten's job was to peel potatoes, and mine to
wash dishes in the galley. Fine, healthy jobs for
a husky bosun's mate, United States Navy, and a

sealing captain, wasn't they? And what harm?
But our particular boss, the head steward, was one
of those cocky little Japs who used to elbow us
out of the alleyways every time he went by. Well"
—Cahalan spat reflectively over the side—"maybe it's true, as some say, that the white race has
seen its best days and the yellow boys are havin'
their turn; but one thing's sure—they're not yet
quite so sure of it that the job sets easy on 'em.
They sure rubbed it into us. Not a meal that we
didn't come near breaking a few large platters over
the heads of some of 'em.

"Anyway, not a harbor we put into that our
heads weren't out the air-ports for signs of the
schooner, and going into Yokohama one fine day
there she lay to moorings in the stream. The
pair of us we could hardly keep from punchin'
each other for excitement, and that night, as our
steamer was about to leave, we slipped ashore.
We hadn't a cent between us, nor clothes enough
to keep us warm; for we'd sold our coats and
flannel shirts for tobacco and a few drinks of
vodka while in jail at Vladivostok. But we beat
the water-front, in the hope of an opening or
meeting up with somebody we knew—but nothing.
If there was only an American cruiser or gun-
boat about—but nothing we could butt in on,
not another American we knew in the place. A

bit discouraged maybe we was, but be sure we had no notion of the *Bounding Boy* getting away without our bein' 'round to see her off.

"First, we needed weapons of some kind. One of those two-handed *samurai* swords wouldn't 've been too bad, but no chance to steal one even; or a piece of lead pipe would 've been a great help. This, mind you, was late in the afternoon of the next day, and we were hungry and growing a little careless of local law. We had no money, as I said, but one of Patten's fingers flew one of those seal rings—you know the kind—wide gold band with a woman's head in some kind of brown stone, looking sideways. 'Say, Cap,' I says, 'you'll have to pawn that.'

" 'What!' yells Patten, 'my birthday gift from Addie!'

"Bein' a birthday gift, I takes a closer look. Sure enough, it was one of those six-carat things with the brown glass which Patten thought was some precious stone. I knew where there used to be a jeweller's window on Eighth Avenue piled high with about twelve dozen gross of them, and you took your pick for four-ninety-eight. On the west coast they might 've cost a dollar more, or maybe two dollars more at Christmas time.

"There was nothing else to do, so I took Patten by the hand and led him to a sort of second-hand curio shop, where was a pair of ancient, double-barrel, percussion-cap pistols in a box that I'd spotted that morning. Long-barrelled things they were, with crossed American flags engraved on the yellow bone grips. How they got there was a mystery—maybe pinched off some American naval officer the time Perry was there. I doubted could we ever get the old things to go off again, and we couldn't try them there because we'd probably get pinched by a division of those little ju-jutsu policemen if we did and they happened to go off. The old fellow runnin' the place finally swapped the pistols for the seal ring; and for my black silk neckerchief, which I was hoping to save for my old mother, he sent a boy out for fresh charges of black powder. The bullets and caps were in the box. I doubted the virtue of the caps, but the pistols would do to put up a bluff.

" 'Twas night by then, and we ready to storm a Japanese battle-ship if only there was a square meal layin' around anywhere on her deck. Well, we sashayed the water-front and cut a sampan adrift, and, paddling out into the stream, made fast to the *Boy's* bobstay and climbed inboard over her bow. In his hurry Patten fell over the windlass, and I thought I heard a scurryin' and a voice from the fo'c's'le under us. I asked Patten if he heard it.

" 'I wonder is my money safe?' was all he answered.

" 'Never mind your money,' I says; 'let's see who's aboard. But first let's take a look at the cabin.'

"We found the door to the cabin locked, so we went back to the fo'c's'le, of which the hatch was but half drawn. By that alone we knew somebody was aboard. We slid the hatch clean back. No light, no noise—which we didn't like. People don't leave a vessel in a harbor without locking her up. We waited, ears and eyes strained for sound or sight of something below. Not a sound; nobody.

"Well, we wouldn't stand there all night. I took off my boots, tucked the old pistols into my waistband, and let myself down the fo'c's'le ladder. And a good job I made of it; they would have needed good ears below to hear me. Once down, I lay behind the ladder for a full five minutes, maybe, before I rapped—two short and three long taps, softly—for Patten to come down. I wanted to tell him to look out, to take his boots off, too, like I did, that the top step of the ladder was slippery with grease; but I didn't dare to speak out loud. It was so dark that I couldn't see him coming; but when he did come a stone image could 've heard him, for, when he threw his weight on that top step, away went those smooth-

soled boots from under him and down he came.
Plump! he hit the fo'c's'le floor. And there he
lay, not a sound out of him, for the longest time
—till I began to think he was dead, had broken his
spine, maybe. I was about to crawl around the
ladder to investigate, when I heard a move and a
sort of groan, and then, from out of the darkness,
the most surprised words: 'Spirits of nitre, but
aren't she deep!'

"I couldn't help it—I had to roar; but hearing
a scrapin' sound then I shut up quick and set to
considerin' again, now that we were below, what
we could do. I remembered that in the schooner
there used to be a lamp in a bracket over the
cook's closet, which ought to be just behind where
I was now layin'. I got up and felt about. Good
enough! There it was, and matches beside it. I
took down the lamp, and, feeling no heat coming
out of the galley stove, opened the oven door,
shoved the lamp in, and lit it. 'Patten,' I whispers then, 'crawl over here.' Which he did, not
quite as smooth and slippery as an eel, but gettin'
over after a while. Then I took the lamp, reached
it out at arm's-length around the stove, and
waited to see what would happen. Nothing. I
took a peep around the after outboard leg of the
stove. So far as the lamp's rays shot out, nothing;
but from somewhere for'ard came a heavy breath-

ing, and we knew that somebody in the peak was getting excited.

" 'An' you'll be more excited yet,' I says to myself, though not oversure that the two of us wouldn't be the most excited of all before it was over with.

"We waited. All at once, bang-g-g! For just a flash the darkness of the peak was lit up. And we could hear the ting of the bullet where it hit the galley tins behind us. 'Twas the lamp they aimed at, for that smashed and the light quivered, flickered, and died out; and in the dark I could feel the lamp oil flowin' against my face where I lay on the floor behind the stove.

" 'Well, they're sure on the job,' I whispers to Patten, and we stayed laid out flat there with our rusty old curios held under the stove and trained forward, both of us wonderin' would they go off at all, even with the fresh powder the old fellow gave us; but no more wonderin' then, for 'twas a sound of cautious steps comin' nearer.

" 'They must be coming over the lockers, Cahalan—from the peak. They're probably wondering if we're armed,' whispers Patten, which was what I was thinkin'; and thinkin', too, that they'd be making a rush soon for the ladder. And if they ever made the deck and slid the hatch it would be all up with us.

The Cruise o' the "Bounding Boy"

" 'They ought to be abreast of the foremast butt now,' whispers Patten a second or two later. 'Will I shoot?'

" 'Not yet, but here—quick!' I whispers back. 'Let me haul off your boots. Here, keep one and I'll take the other. Now rake the lockers, you to port and me to starboard—now!' And we stood up and let go with a full swing, each of us a heavy sealer's boot. One went bouncing for'ard into the peak; from one side to the other we could hear it. The other had better luck, for it was a most surprised grunt we heard, as if it had fetched up awfully sudden on somethin' human.

"We were almost laughing to ourselves to think of how that broadside o' boots must 've surprised 'em, when, bang-g-g! bang-g-g! bang-g-g! one, two, three revolvers at least—eight, ten, or a dozen bullets, most of them hittin' against the stove, but two or three ricochetting along the floor and among the galley tins behind.

"After that we lay without a stir for what we reckoned was five minutes. 'You listen and I'll groan,' says I to Patten, then, 'and I'll bet they'll light a lamp and take a look around, for they must be sure by now we've got no guns.' And so it happened. We could only see the hand of whoever lit the table lamp as he reached around— a brown hand and wrist. With a service revolver

I could have whipped that hand off—even with the old muzzle-loader I was tempted to try it, but didn't. Instead, I took to groaning, and Patten lay like one dead. We'd already given up the notion of making any bluff with our ancient duellos. We were glad to be still alive. Our feet stuck out beyond the stove and they might have been seen there, but hardly more than that of us as they came out from the peak again. Squinting under the stove we could see them; four of them, creeping over the lockers toward us. Sure enough, the leader of the four was our old cook. 'D' y' see him—Zippy?' breathed Patten—and he was wild. 'Well, I'm goin' to wing him—watch!' and takes aim with his ancient duelling pistol. But it didn't go off. He snaps the other barrel. No report. Zippy raises his revolver at the second click—he had stopped dead after the first click—and I made up my mind to take a chance at him. No time for loafin'. 'And if she don't go off,' I says to Patten, 'we'll jump up and give 'em a broadside of stove covers.' For all my hurry, I takes a good long squint through the sights at Zippy—the sights were all right and, glory be! the old muzzle-loader went off, and Zippy, after swinging a little to one side and hangin' uncertain for about four seconds, sagged gently in the middle and fell off the lockers as loose as any sack o' commissary beans ever you see tumbled into the hold. The other three then stopped short as if they didn't know what to do.

"'Zippy,'" calls out Patten then, 'tell your people to hold their hands above their heads.' But no answer of word or action came to that.

"'Zippy,' I calls out then, and I tries to give a good imitation of myself pipin' a lazy watch the length of a battle-ship's 'tween-decks. 'Zippy, my boy, you're not dead, and don't try to make out you are. But you will be in about three seconds if you don't tell them what Captain Patten just ordered—and hurry!'

"Zippy's voice was heard then, and the three others lifted high their hands, at which we crawled out from behind the galley stove and took their guns from them and drove 'em into bunks, and motioned them to turn their faces toward the ship's side, which they did.

"'Now,' says Patten, 'we'll go aft on that little treasure hunt.'

"'No,' says I, 'we'll just have a bite to eat— nothing since eight o'clock last night, and I'm hungry.'

"'That's right,' says Patten. 'I'm hungry, too,' and we foraged the galley and had a great meal. 'Now for the money,' says Patten and went up the ladder, and soon I could hear him kicking in the cabin door. In may be a quarter of an hour he was back. No need to ask was the money gone.

" 'What 'll we do?' he asks, all discouraged; at which I saw the man lacked imagination, and so took charge myself.

" 'First, let's lift this Zippy man into a bunk,' I said, and we did. 'But not your face to the wall,' I adds to Zippy. 'Now, you loafer, you look and listen and answer questions.' And taking his revolver I broke it open, emptied the cylinder, looked the cartridges over, slid the two good ones back, snapped the cylinder into place, all very deliberate, and very deliberately took a seat on the locker beside the bunk he lay in and placed the muzzle against his head.

" 'Now, Zippy, my friend,' I says, 'take a good look at me—me, Mister Cahalan, bosun's mate, first class, United States Navy. No, no, straight at me—if you can.' And he did, or as straight as a cross-eyed Jap could. 'You know me? Don't speak—just bow your head.' He bowed his head. 'Sure?' He bowed again; pretty respectful, too. 'Well, in one, two, say ten—no, five seconds after I give the word I'm goin' to know where Captain Patten's money is, or your soul will be on the way to whatever kind of Jap hell is comin' to you. If you don't know, that 'll be your hard luck—you go just the same. Now, think fast. Wait till we start even. Now! One —two-o—three-e—four-r—f——"

" 'There—under there—deep down,' says Zippy, and points to a barrel of flour among the galley stores. Patten jumped to the flour barrel, but I had to lean back to press my fingers to my throat, which had tightened up some. For just a second I was wonderin' would Zippy call my little bluff, and then what would I done? Would I shoot? I dunno.

"Patten yelled out loud—his money was there. So far all right. We lifted Zippy on deck, had him call up his chums, made 'em make sail for us, then put them all in the sampan, took it in tow, and headed out the harbor. Ten miles out to sea we turned the sampan adrift. An hour after daylight old white-headed Fujiyama was horizon down, and the *Bounding Boy* laying out a sweet ten-and-a-half knots for Puget Sound, and for Puget Sound we kept her headed, and never a heave-to till we were to anchor at Seattle again."

Cahalan paused in his narrative and surveyed the quarter-deck below. The doings of that same group of young ladies who had won his attention at the beginning of his story seemed to have caught his attention. There was a blue-clad, delightful one who particularly won his admiration.

"And even that one," commented Cahalan:
"Patten 'd 've given her thirty days in the brig—
and ten days of it on bread and water—just for the
crime of her ugliness beside his battle-ship beauty
—just because he happened to see her first. I'm
not so much blamin' him for that, but I do blame
him for not havin' sense enough to allow for the
natural bias after bein' a year to sea. Every man
has a bias somewhere that he must allow for, or
bang! goes his rating. But that man! A man
forty-five year old and no more judgment than—
than"—he looked about for an extremely illumi-
nating comparison—"than any o' those apprentice
boys loafin' under the turret there."

"But he saw her again?" we asked him.

"Saw her!" snorted Cahalan. "He ran all the
way up from the dock—and his money with him.
And me"—he rubbed his chin and grinned slyly
—"me after him."

"And she was at Tagen's still?"

"She was. His golden-haired Amazonian Addie,
she was there, but not now cashiering behind any
cage. Not Addie, no, sir. She was married
now, and her and her husband between them
owned the hotel and the bar and the restaurant;
and the new landlord wasn't sitting in his shirt-
sleeves readin' the morning paper in his office.
Not him. And his head bartender and his res-

taurant cashier wasn't doin' business without any cash registers."

"And Tagen ?"

"Oh, Tagen was workin' for another man down the street. And"—Cahalan sighed—"he must 've done a great business, Tagen, in the old place, to stand the drainage long's he did. For, besides the seven months we'd been gone on our cruise, they'd had the run of the place for two years before that."

"And what did the lady have to say to Patten ?"

"Well, there stood Patten afore the desk, and there was Addie behind it. She'd about forgotten him, anybody could see, but she gave him one of her mechanical smiles and introduced him to her husband, our old friend the smooth Johnnie, and Patten went out to the bar and hoisted whiskies into him, ten or twelve, till he got a cryin' jag on, and then his old friend Johnnie said that maybe he'd better go; and Patten went and me with him, but not till I'd given Johnnie one sweet one under the ear for old acquaintance' sake—a beaut— and he was still falling backward across the floor when I ran out after Patten, for of course I had to stand by him now. At every other step I kept telling him he was the luckiest dog alive not to be married to her. But no use—no use to tell him that in a little while the pair of them would be sitting up nights tryin' to trim each other. Couldn't he see it for himself? But he couldn't, nor that his thousand dollars in the minin' scheme was well worth it, if with it he got rid of him. And so all the way along the street till he comes to a gamblin' joint, and there he goes in and drops all the money he had rescued from Zippy except what he'd given me. And what harm but I had to try it with my twelve hundred dollars— my share, double wages—the same that I'd intended to take home, or the most of it, anyway, to my good old mother in Brooklyn. But now I lays half of it down, and wins. And lays what I'd won, six hundred dollars, down, and wins again. Good. Now I had twenty-four hundred dollars, and, happenin' to think that with twice that I'd have enough to buy the old lady one of those Jersey bungalows I used to see advertised in the New York Sunday papers she used to send me, I laid down the whole twenty-four hundred. 'That red water-line color still looks good to me —let 'em come,' I says, and the whole house stands by to look. And"—Cahalan looked mournfully up to the sky—"they let 'em come."

"And?"

"And-d?" Cahalan beautifully imitated the inquiring note of the persistent questioner. "I'm here and still a bosun's mate. And my old mother

The Cruise o' the "Bounding Boy"

is still living in the middle of a three-decker in Brooklyn with twelve Lithuanians topside and a family named Wyzinski on the deck below."

And just then a good sea-going bugler poised himself in the bulkhead doorway and sounded mess-gear, and what more was there to say?

THE SEA-FAKER

The Sea-Faker

A LONG time since I had landed on that particular dock, and so it happened that now, for the first time in years, I saw him. No other passengers took any particular notice of him; and no reason, not knowing his history, why they should, unless it were to mark the humor, or pathos, of the situation—the short, fat man in the company's uniform who was so terribly busy driving people toward the two lines of rope converging to the West Street gate—a fussy, whiskered man, the whiskers untrimmed, uncombed, tobacco-stained; a man with a vanishing shade of a once-fresh complexion and a rather weak-kneed reminder of a seaman's rolling gait.

Well, here's about him:

There was a passenger steamer, one of the biggest of her day, running between Liverpool and New York; and one west-bound trip she ran ashore off Sambro Head—off Halifax, that is. If you have been a student of maritime affairs and are not too young, you will know at once what wreck is meant; if not, or if it was before your time, you will need to be told something of it.

It was the most disgraceful disaster in steamship history. There were nine hundred passengers on that ship. Six hundred were lost. Nine hundred passengers, and not one woman passenger saved; and only one child—a little boy whose uncle took him on his back and swam ashore with him. The ship's company were saved—that is, pretty much. Probably nobody at all would have been saved but for a seaman who took a line when she struck and carried it to the lighthouse people on the beach. He was that same little boy's uncle.

Now, directing the course of the ship at the time was a pilot, but on the bridge also was a ship's officer. The pilot was giving the course to the man at the wheel, when the ship's officer changed it. The pilot protested, but the watch officer was one of those men who know it all. He butted in again, and up on the rocks went the big liner. It was thick of snow at the time and a cold night. Those of the six hundred who were not drowned were frozen to death.

The investigation which followed cleared the pilot and broke the second officer, though breaking him was little consolation to the families of those six hundred drowned people. Very little.

Some one may ask if that is all that ever happened. It is. That's maritime law. Queer kinks in maritime law. If a motorman should run over your child, or anybody else, drunk or sober, you can send him to jail; but the drunken or incompetent ship's officer can lose a thousand lives, and all that happens to him is that he loses his job. Lots of other funny little things about marine laws.

But to get back to the wreck. It happened that the man at the wheel was a fellow named Batkins, who had served many a year before the mast, served his time over and over, and might have been serving it yet only for that wreck. They summoned him as a witness in the investigation; and he lied for them; lied not intelligently, but stubbornly, stolidly — by the hour. He had heard nothing, seen nothing, knew nothing of this officer's interference with the pilot. What he said was controverted by the other man on the bridge, the man who later swam ashore with the line. They believed the other fellow, sustained the pilot and broke the ship's officer; but Batkins had established himself with the company as the kind of a servant they wanted, and not long after he was quietly made a fourth officer. The sea man who told the truth was fired. So far as this story is concerned, no further matter what became of him. He was an adventurer, anyway, and one berth fitted him as well as another. No need to worry about him, but I might say that he was my uncle and I the little boy he swam ashore with. This is to explain how I came to know so much about that wreck; and also how I came to keep track of Batkins.

To get on: Now we have Batkins the subordinate officer; and a good subordinate he was, as subordinates are measured in his company's office. He had committed perjury to help out the company, and when by any chance he was called into the office he showed by his words and bearing that the company's law was his law—always. And he salved the vanity of the company's topsiders beautifully by the way he kotowed; and he didn't put that part of it on. No hypocrisy in that. He just naturally believed that some people were born to high places and others to low places. He came from that kind of people. If he had been born on some gentleman's estate up in middle England instead of down near the Liverpool docks, then, no doubt of it, he would have made the finest kind of an under-servant. People with souls like that do sometimes take to the sea and rise to command, but, thank the Lord, not too often.

Well, Batkins was promoted. Third, second, first officer; and, in time, the company developing and new ships building fast, he gets his command. And hardly does he get his command than he happens along while a ship, a tramp steamer, is sinking in mid-ocean, and takes off her crew. That is, there being a little sea on, he calls for volunteers; and a nervy fellow, his third officer, jumps into a boat with half a dozen men and they row over and take her crew off. Coming alongside, the skipper of the sinking ship has his leg broken, and between that and the long exposure on his wrecked ship he dies aboard Captain Batkins ship even as his own ship goes down.

That striking incident, the taking of people off a leaking ship in mid-ocean, impressed the passengers (the mid-ocean touch always does impress people), and that captain dying as his own ship went down tempted the newspapers, and they played it up in great shape; made terrible weather of it—a gale of wind and mountainous seas—and in the storm-centre of it all they put the "calm-eyed Captain Batkins."

And he was given a banquet and loving-cup, and he made a speech. You can picture him as he stood up to make his speech, one hand stilling the applause and the other clutching his wineglass. "No, no, gentlemen, it is not for me to say I am a hero. What man, indeed, can say that of himself? But as one of a small corps of men leading lives of—k-h-m—well, continual peril, as one might say, one—k-h-m—one learns to look on such things as

part of the day's work. And after all, gentlemen, I only done my duty." Whereat another pop-
eyed imbecile jumped up and thanked God there
were still men who knew how to do their duty.
And the band played, and there was cheering
enough to call the policeman in from his beat.

Now, at the end of the head table was young
Willie Carrick. Willie had been invited because
of his father, and I had gone because Willie had
asked me to, and now Willie blurted out—he
couldn't help it, "Will somebody tell me what
that fat-necked pickerel did that was heroic?"
"What's that?" asked half a dozen horrified ones.
"What's what?" snapped Willie. "As near as I
can make out he stood on the bridge while another
lot of chaps got into a boat and did the job. Fifty
feet above the water-line he was, taking about as
much chance as if he was on the quarter-deck of
a Broadway trolley car in a shower of rain.
Where's the third officer who took them off in
the lifeboat?—that's what I want to know."

"But his superb seamanship!" says one.

"Superb slop," says Willie. "Turning a ship
around? Why, every time my chauffeur turns his
car around he's doing a damn sight more difficult
job, for he hasn't the whole ocean to turn it in.
And more dangerous, for if he doesn't look out
some trolley car will come along and bump him

good. What in the devil did he do?" asks Willie again.

"But it *was* rough weather, Mr. Carrick?"

"Rough, was it? It couldn't have been too rough for a big ship when a thirty-foot boat lived in it, could it? No? Then what in the devil did he do?"

And when they came to think it over, a lot of them there, being moderately intelligent men, wanted to know what he did do after all. But no matter—by that time the papers had printed full reports of the dinner, and Batkins was a great fellow. And the advertising didn't do the company any harm.

Well, some time afterward Willie and I were slated to go to the Mediterranean together, but Willie got me to wait till Miss Kaylor and her mother were going; which was all right, only they happened to take passage on Batkins's ship. "Lord, Lord!" groaned Willie, but there was nothing for us but to go on her just the same.

We had kept track of Batkins, but it was the first time we had either of us seen him to speak to since the presentation; and he had already grown into one of those captains that you have to have a letter of introduction to every time you meet him, unless you were of important people—like Willie. When he spied Willie it was, "Oh, Mr. Carrick!

Come up here, won't you?" It was from the bridge he called out, just after he dropped the pilot. But Willie walked back down the promenade deck pretending not to have heard him. "The big sausage!" said Willie. "I s'pose we'll have to spend half our time trying to dodge him now."

But Willie could not dodge him—Willie's father had too large a say in the company's affairs. That very evening he had us into his cabin. There were five or six other passengers there, Miss Kaylor and her mother among them. The famous loving-cup was on a table in the centre of the room, and, naturally, somebody had to ask him about it. And he swung around on his swivel chair and started right in. "A plain seaman's yarn," he said, by way of beginning, and then he went on. That yarn had grown and grown; so that if he had only had a little more imagination, he would have made an epic of the sea of it. Not only that night, but every night after dinner it was the same —the choice company invited into the captain's cabin and somebody sure to ask about the cup, and then Batkins starting in on the story. By this time he had been talking about it three years steadily, and the tears, especially if he had three or four highballs in him, used to come to his eyes as he went on.

The Sea-Faker

We used to study him, Carrick and myself, when we had nothing better to do. Mind you, aboard ship he was a great man. No kotowing here the same as when he went up to the company's office to report. Remember that for thirty years or more he had been buckling under to somebody else, but no more of that now. He's captain now. No longer does he have to stand four hours' watch in a dry nor'west blizzard, cold enough to freeze your marrow, nor in a north-east snow-storm slushy enough to keep you from breathing almost. No longer does he have to turn out for any night watch or morning watch unless he feels like it. No more the stress of duty which might have kept the salt in his blood and the marrow in his bones. He just does not have to do anything now that he doesn't feel like doing, except stand on the bridge with the pilot leaving port and going into port, and he probably liked to do that.

Mornings he used to walk down the promenade deck, and never would Carrick see him coming but he would begin to jibe. "Here's his game," Carrick would say, "on these fine sunny mornings, when the sea-dogs of saloon passengers are stretched out in their steamer-chairs with rugs to their chins and books in their laps. See him now? He's stoppin' and speakin' here and there, to those he thinks worth while, and that's what pleases 'em. But do you know what I think, Boynton?" We were leaning over the rail—a beautiful day and the fascinating Azores ahead. "I think he's trying to make a hit with the old lady—with Mrs. Kaylor, yes." Mrs. Kaylor was a widow with a few millions and Batkins was a widower.

"No, no, Willie—he's too raw to attract her, too raw."

"Don't you be too sure. This is her third trip on this ship. Do you know what she was saying to me yesterday after he'd done his promenade? 'Why, the idea of that bluff old sea-dog who faces the perils of the sea, the man on whose courage and seamanship may depend all our lives—why, to think of that old sea-dog stopping in the midst of his tremendous responsibilities and talking about ordinary things, isn't it wonderful?' I think she's getting soft over him—yes. The day before he told her his stock story of Davy Jones's locker, wriggling his eyebrows while he was telling it—and why, he was just the delightfulest, jolliest, drollest old sea dog ever was—yes. What do green young things like you and me know what an impressionable woman will do when she's caught on her romantic side? The day before that, the rainy day, when he walked along the deck in his dripping sou'wester and slicker, the sea-water drippin' from his whiskers, why she knew he was the stuff heroes are made of. Yes, indeed; did he not look it? How'd you like to be sitting in the next chair and have to listen to his tales of the danger of crossing the Atlantic? Danger—in a ship this size! About as dangerous as crossing Central Park in a rowboat! But his getting away with it—the old sausage!"

The Kaylors' and Carrick's chairs were together, which gave Batkins, when he got through buzzing Mrs. Kaylor, a chance to talk to Carrick, if he and Miss Kaylor hadn't escaped when his back was turned. When Carrick got caught like that he would fly distress signals, at which I used to send hurry-up messages to him and Miss Kaylor from the other end of the deck. And Miss Kaylor used to be very grateful, though sometimes she thought she ought to stand guard by mamma. When her conscience pained her like that, Willie would leave her and join me in the chief engineer's room.

The chief, Carrick, and I had met before, and the chief would make a cup of tea in the afternoon or maybe have down a bottle of stout of an evening, when we used to sit in on him till he had to turn in; but he would sit up late enough at that.

The chief, Gifford his name, was quite a chap. We had both known him a long time. He was not the regular chief engineer of the ship. In fact, he hated the ship and had no use for her master, and was forever bewailing the luck which had sent him aboard, even for this one trip. "When the people that know the least about a man tell you he is a great chap, and those that know the most about him tell you he is an awful fake, then you want to watch out for him," says Gifford. An outspoken man, Gifford, with a great pride in his profession. "On sailin'-ships look for the men handlin' the sails; on steamers look for the men in charge o' the steam. These heroes o' the bridge, they're makin' a laughin' stock o' us in the eyes o' them that knows. A pilot takes us out o' port on one end and a pilot takes us into port on the other, and there's three thousand miles o' clear water in between. Where's the danger, barrin' collision, so long as we c'n keep our steam up?"

"It's fair sickenin'," went on Gifford another day, "to listen to some o' them. I'm namin' no names; but here we are, one o' the biggest ships afloat, and now and again we run through a gale o' wind an' a bit o' sea. Two trips ago and that was the case, and what followed? Why, the passengers they gets together and pass resolutions testifyin' to the heroism and seamanship o' the captain and officers. Why, man, there was never a sea came out o' the ocean can hurt a 5,000-ton ship— not 'less they're drunk or foolish on the bridge, or, o' course, somethin's gone wrong below. It makes me fair sick, the foolishness o' them. Why, if we're heroes, then what about those little fishin' smacks we passes on the Banks? Why, they're not a hundred feet in len'th, most of 'em, an' their rail no higher out o' water than that," and Gifford put his hand on a level with his knee, "an' they're out there through all the gales that ever blew. An' if we're heroes—five, six, seven hundred feet long—what o' them? Their very mast-heads no higher than our bridge—what o' them? They ha' no ten or twenty or forty thousand horsepower. They ha' to fight the wind wi' the power o' the wind itself, an' they do. And if we're heroes, what o' them? But they're real sailors an' won't stand for that kind o' gush, but it's spoilin' us. No, sir, no harm can come to a good-sized steamer on the ocean these days 'less by collision—not if she's well found."

"Well, this one is well found," says Carrick, "and thank God for it!"

"Is she?" Gifford looked at Carrick. "Wi' all due respect to you, Mr. Carrick, an' your father's property—she could be better found."

"What's wrong?" asked Carrick.

"What's always wrong if there's nobody to watch out? When the old company sold out to you they sold you many a ship that needs overhaulin'. But there's no need to worry—an' here's Ned."

Ned was Baldwin, the third officer then, but second officer at this time, who had done the rescue work for which Captain Batkins, as commander, had been given the loving cup.

"Suppose I go down now and look at that boiler-bed," said Baldwin. "Maybe I can dig out some gear to strap it down with."

"A little thing wrong in the boiler-room," explained Gifford, and went off with Baldwin.

We were all in our bunks that night when there set in a gale which stayed with us for two days and nights. And after the wind came the sea. The ship was rolling unaccountably at times, and as rumors were creeping around the deck withal, Carrick and I thought that perhaps we had better go down and have a word with our friend, the chief engineer, even though we knew he would be busy.

There was surely something wrong, and Carrick was becoming worried for the safety of Miss Kaylor and her mother. He wanted to bring them, if not a reassuring, at least an intelligent message. "But maybe Gifford or Baldwin will tell us something," he said.

Gifford was not in his usual place, and no sign of Baldwin. So we went below, and came on them back-to. "I give you steam and you can't keep her head-to—what's wrong?" Gifford was saying. "She's kept head-to when I'm on the bridge all right," answered Baldwin.

At this time the ship was in the trough of the sea and rolling over, and even while we were finding our way down the iron ladders she rolled so far over that we thought she was going on her beam ends. But she did not; but before she had done she rolled far enough down to loosen her boiler-heads. Carrick and I were there when it happened—no joke that. No; but she was still one of the biggest ships afloat and she would have to fill up before she would go down. And no great danger of that as yet; though if her boilers were not secured again there was danger of their piling through the side of the ship. That would have fixed her, of course. But there was the chief engineer on the job and a couple of good assistants. They were there to prevent a thing like that, or anything like it. And they were doing it.

A day and a night before Gifford and his force got things straightened out through it all. Carrick stayed, only leaving to carry calming messages to Miss Kaylor and her mother. And things were now looking so right we thought we would soon be on our way again, when this something else happened. Her boiler and engine room suddenly began to fill up. In short order it was a foot deep, and that forced Gifford to draw his fires and ease off his steam, and with that the ship at once fell into the trough of the sea and began to roll. She had been rolling some before, but now she began to roll for fair. A dozen times or so we thought she would roll over entirely. And water, water, nothing but water in her engine and boiler rooms, and mounting higher. Gifford was working like a fiend. At last he felt sure it was not a leaky seam, but a broken valve. There was so much loose water in her that they could not see what was doing underneath, but Gifford placed the cause at last and roused out his division and put them on the job. "Go down there, you bullies," he yells, "an' hunt for that hole, and when you find it plug it up—and good and tight!" And down they went, and you can imagine them—stripped to their waists, all black with coal-dust and muck, and the black sea-water rising higher and higher about them. And then comes Baldwin with a message from the skipper. "Somebody's been to him with a tale of how things are going down here— he's talking of the boats," says Baldwin.

"The boats—good God, man!" exploded Gifford. "We've drifted out o' the track o' steamers and we're a hundred miles or so off shore. We've a full complement—three thousand souls aboard—

an' the boats won't hold more than a third o' the passengers."

"I told him all that and, further, that the boats wouldn't live twenty-four hours—that another storm was comin'."

"An' what did he say?"

"He said, 'And who said there's to be a storm?' 'My judgment, sir,' I answers. And he says, 'Is your judgment or mine to prevail on this ship?'"

"Go back," says Gifford, "an' tell him we'll be all right in an hour or two, but don't let him come down if you c'n stop him!" And Baldwin starts back, but meets his captain on the way to the engine-room.

And Gifford—without sleep for three days and nights now—Gifford, black-faced and red-eyed, waited his captain's coming. "Aye, you're comin' —an' for what good? A good seaman you may ha' been once, but what now? How long since you stood a full watch—the very marrow o' your soul gone to rot! No more than the head porter of a floatin' hotel you've become! Aye, an' more of us will become flunkys like you if we don't watch out."

So Gifford waits, sullen as could be. And down the ladder comes Batkins. Soft and flabby enough he looked. A long time since he was faced with a man's work, and now his eyes roamed uncertainly. He and the chief engineer had not hit it off well from the hour they left the dock. There was a look in this temporary chief engineer's eyes that Batkins didn't quite like.

Captain Batkins was standing on the grating now and looking down. It was pretty black down there and he did not take it all in at once; but when he did, when he saw below him those stokers, a lot of black, naked devils, plunging one after the other into the sea-water, and the sea-water, black as ink most of it, rushing, just rushing in from some hole or whatever it was through the ship's side, and getting higher and higher and it then to the men's waists, he rolls his eyes and yells, "We're lost! My God, we're lost! The boats!" like somebody on the stage.

And the chief, directing his men, looks across at him and yells, "What!" And the men look up and see who it is—the captain himself. Great Lord, where the captain quits! Not a word out of them, but like one man they jump for the ladders and the free air, where a man could fight for his life when she went down. They would have got away too, only the chief picks up a spanner or something, long as your arm, and catches the first chap a crack over the head, and the second man, and the third, and the fourth, and the fifth, and says, "Now, you whelps' sons, go down and finish that job!" And they, more afraid of the chief and his long, heavy spanner than any other kind of sudden death just then, they drop below and begin to paw around in that black mess again. And the chief turns to Baldwin and says, "Ned, what d' y' say if we take that old granny an' lock him up? Law's law, of course, an' discipline's discipline, but three thousand lives they're worth more than my ticket an' yours. What d' y' say?" And Baldwin stops to think. Being a bridge officer is a little different from being in the engine-room in a matter like that; but Carrick breaks in, "Yes, why don't you?" at which Baldwin says, "Maybe it's the only thing to do, after all," and grabs the skipper and hustles him into the chief's room.

Now, somebody may ask, but wasn't that mutiny? It was, assault and battery added, for Baldwin threw him into the room any old way. And Carrick helped. "In with you, you overfed bologna!" And if you'd seen Batkins looking at Carrick when he heard that!

They kept Batkins locked up till it was time to take the bridge going into port. And he wasn't too thick-witted to see where it left him; for not only the engineer's but some of the deck force had seen him hustled away, and when they reached the home port he preferred charges against Gifford and Baldwin—to save his face, that was. And the company, which had to go on record as standing behind its own captain, backed him up.

Gifford and Baldwin were put ashore; but no need to worry about them. Carrick saw to it that their story reached headquarters. He felt immensely grateful to them for showing Batkins up. "Imagine that Cheshire cheese for a father-in-law!" he said, and saw to it that they were assigned to the next new ship which went into commission, which was all they wanted. Batkins could have the name, but give them the good billets.

As very few of the passengers really knew what happened—Carrick wasn't knocking his own father's property—the company gave out a fine story about the last great work of their favorite captain, one of their old and tried servants, and he became a hero again. And to drown the noise of a queer kind of rumor that something about the wreck wasn't all right, they gave him another banquet and another cup, and he made another speech, and the public forgot the rumor. And when they had also forgotten a lot about him, the company quietly shifted him to a freighter, to bring up the standard of the freight service, they explained; and after he had been there awhile they even more unobtrusively gave him a shore job where he couldn't do any harm, and after another period they dropped him off the pay-roll entirely.

The Sea-Faker

And then he went to the bad. Drink, mostly. And it was Carrick who took him out of the gutter and made his father give him the job he's now got. On days when he isn't marshalling passengers between the lines of rope, you can find him out at the West Street entrance armed with a long stick. His job there is to keep the irreverent West Side boys from invading the sacred precincts. Every now and then, Carrick says, some old passengers see him and, recollecting him, take him out to dinner, and then—especially if he gets two or three highballs into him—the old fellow spouts of his great days as an ocean-liner commander. And once in a while he is written up in the newspapers, which call attention to him once more, and "What a great chap he must have been!" you can hear somebody say. And it is possible that he himself believes by this time that he was a great man once.

The word hero is still a fine word; but I never read about one of these steamship heroes that I don't wonder if he's a Batkins. I know that there are plenty of fine steamship commanders—plenty of them, of the finest; but we don't see that kind standing for a two-column write-up after every breeze of wind they come through—not when his ship is six or seven hundred feet long.

HEROES

Heroes

DINNIE tucked the stowaway under the blanket. "Squeeze in by the ship's side, b'y. That's it—that's the good b'y. But will you"—Dinnie turned to his mate—"take a look at the size of him, Geordie?"

Geordie took a look. "Oh, aye, Dinnie," and went off in a roar. "The littleness 'f 'im, Dinnie. And stowed away in there—ho, ho, Dinnie!—'e's like, like the larst little bloater in the corner o' the box!"

"'Tis more a sardine size I'd say he was, Geordie. But he'll be all right soon. Won't you, b'y? Sure you will. That's the lad. Look at the shmile of him now, Geordie."

"Ay, but so frightened like, Dinnie."

"And why wouldn't he be?—not knowin' what's goin' to happen to him, the poor lad. But wouldn't you think, Geordie, *wouldn't* you think now, when his father died in survice, as you might say, they'd be givin' the lad a free passage home? But no matther now. We've got him through the furst night annyway, and who knows

239

maybe we'll get him all the way across and no ship's officer the wiser. 'Twould be fine, though, could we be payin' the passage money oursel's, wouldn't it, Geordie? Sure and it would; but we couldn't hardly be doin' that on our wages. But maybe we'd betther be goin' below, Geordie. And till we be comin' back"—he held a finger up to the stowaway—"no n'ise, b'y, no n'ise."

"Ay, lad," affirmed Geordie, "no noise, lad; for it's watch and watch, y' know, and when we goes they comes. And not always in the best bloody temper. Four hours of 'eavin coal into a row of bloody fire-boxes—it don't go to the makin' of a 'eavenly temper, do it, Dinnie?"

"Har-r-dly, Geordie, har-r-dly. But let us go below now."

II

AWAY down below in that boiler compartment next the bottom of the ship Dinnie and Geordie shovelled and raked, sliced and panted and sweated. Good workers this pair. No need for the watch officer to bother them; but there were those who had to be driven, who staggered and swayed as they worked, and gave much back talk, which made for bad feeling. It may have been that they were still weak, or it may have been that they intended to do no more for the company than they had to; perhaps just off a drunk. Perhaps so. However, now in the first morning watch of the trip they looked gray and sick, and staggered between furnaces.

An hour and a half of steady going and Geordie stepped over for a drink of water, and as he was drinking a steward looked in for the engineer on watch, who happened not to be there just then. Now stewards are a superior class aboard ship. Naturally.

Conversation between the two classes is not always sweet-tempered, but now and then a trusting stoker hopes to meet a civil steward, as now. "Hi s'y, stooard, is 't foggy as they say outside?" asked Geordie, very politely.

"Hi don't know 'ow foggy they said it was," replied the steward wittily, and rushed off.

"You don't? Well, blarst your bloody heyes, if you'll come back 'ere hi'll tell you—an' mike soup of the hair you're breathin' so 'aughtily."

Dinnie touched his chum's arm. "Don't be mindin' the likes o' him, Geordie. A steward! Sure what's a steward?"

"That's right, maties, what's a steward?"

They peered at him. Sure enough it was the young New Yorker Cummings, who had helped them smuggle the young lad aboard. "Now we people"—he waved an easy hand—"have to shovel like coolies and sweat like horses, but there 're *some* things we don't have to do. No man, just because he happens to have the price of a saloon passage, can say to us, 'Here, damn your eyes, where's my shaving water this morning?' And when saloon he feels a bit sea-sick and heaves his last meal any old place, it's not us that has to get down on our knees like a wet nurse and— But you haven't got the makin's, have you?"

Dinnie passed over the paper and tobacco and Cummings began to roll a cigarette, talking easily meanwhile. "I wouldn't mind havin' the money, though, that some of those guys get in tips. It'd be me for a few of the gay European metropolises between trips, you betcher. But, jee-zooks! what's the use?"

Dinnie watched him in admiration. "You're the furst lad ever I see could roll one of them things with one hand an' kape on talkin' with the other."

"Well, that's something, I suppose—even if I don't ever get a medal for anything else. But you were asking that classy steward if it was still foggy. Geordie, was it? Well, it's just as foggy now as it's been all night. And what do you know about that—full speed all night in the fog?"

Heroes

"H-m—it's little you know of the ways of ocean liners, I'm thinkin'."

"Don't forget we're between Sandy Hook and Nantucket, where we're liable any minute to pick up a coaster or a fisherman or another steamer on our bow." He drew the tip of his tongue along the edge of his cigarette-paper. "And why is it?" He caught the string of the tobacco bag and drew it tight in his teeth. "Yes, why do they do it?" He lifted a small hot coal with a bit of waste and held it to his cigarette—puff, puff—he inhaled the smoke, held it a moment, and sent it flying through his nose. "It's against the law, isn't it? Then why do they do it?"

"I'll tell you why, b'y. We has to be at the Azores, d' y' see, on next Thursdah mornin'—say Thursdah early."

"And why early?"

"So the passengers can have their day ashore. And we has to be at Gibraltar on the followin' Mondah mornin' early, so the passengers can have their day ashore agin. If the passengers— tourists, d' y' see—don't have their allowance of time ashore they'll be sayin', 'What the divil kind of a line is this that don't give us time to see all these fine places they advertise?' And so when they falls behind they hasn't it in them to make it up ever. *Comfort*—and *safety*—'tis all in the little books they gives out. Y' ought to read one some time, b'y. They're insthructive—and amusin'. And not havin' the speed to spare, we can't be slowin' down, d' y' see? And so full tilt through the fog we has to go."

"H-m—and some day there'll be a fine mess, won't there? And—jee-zooks! what's that?" He reached his free arm out for support. "Jee-zooks! d' y' see that?" he ejaculated, and snapping his half-smoked cigarette across the deck he bolted for the ladder.

III

Dinnie and Geordie gripped each other. A great bump it was, with one side of the fire-room deck rising high and a lot of coal in the bunkers on that same side tumbling down.

"Faith and 'twill save some coal-passin' that," said Dinnie. Then the tearing and grinding of the ship's plates outside. More coal fell on the deck and thin splashes of sea-water; and then— from above their heads, from above the coal-pile— came sea-water in great sheets.

The flying New Yorker took another backward look. "Twenty feet below the water-line, no place for me—jee-zooks, no!" and continued after the rest of the fire-room gang, who, having hove away shovels, slice-bars, whatever they had in their hands, were rushing for the upper regions. Some went out by the bulkhead door and into the passageway, but most of them jumped for the narrow iron ladder, where immediately was a congestion, with haulings and elbowings, mixed language, and the appearance for a time as if nobody would ever get clear.

Cummings was the last of the crowd to the ladder, and, having to wait for those before and above him, took time for another look about the fire-room. Just two men there. Hauling the fires out from under the boilers they were. Already they had cleaned out two. From where the inrushing water was creeping over the heaps of red coal the steam was ascending in clouds.

To Cummings it seemed that these two men did not realize their danger. "The ship's side is all stove in," he called out.

They paid no attention. "They don't hear me," thought Cummings, and thrust his head forward for a better view. "Why, if it ain't Dinnie and Geordie!" and megaphoned through his hands. "Hey there, you people, come on! They'll nobody pin any medals on you for that—come on!"

But they continued to work feverishly. Even while the New Yorker was warning them they had cleared out another fire-box. "Jee-zooks!"

said Cummings, and having by now a clear ladder-way set his foot on a rung and from there looked back once more. "They're sure a couple of lobsters," he muttered, but waited nevertheless; and, waiting, noticed that the water was up to his shoe-tops. He drew another deep breath, took another look up the ladder, and "Jee-zooks!" he groaned, and slipped over and yelled in Dinnie's ear, "What do I do?"

Dinnie looked around. Cummings thought the stoker would be surprised, but he didn't seem to be. "Hulloh, b'y!" was his cheerful greeting. "Do what we're doin'—haul the fires. And wurk fasht, b'y—wurk fasht."

Cummings began to haul out the hot coals, too. And hauled them fast. It was the only safe way. The outrushing heat, he thought, would shrivel up his insides, while outside it was as if his flesh would blister under the uprising steam. One fire-box, another, and the sea-water was half-way to his knees. He looked around to see how his chums were making out. They were hardly to be seen through the steam, but it encouraged him to see that they, too, had to turn away their heads before the uprush of it.

The fires were all hauled, and Cummings, conceiving his work to be over, made for the ladder. But they did not follow, and looking around again

"And wurk fasht, b'y—wurk fasht"

he saw them turning wheels, and presently heard a tremendous racket. "More trouble!" groaned Cummings. "Not through yet?" he called out.

"No, b'y, we must ease off the shteam yet," and hurriedly turned another valve. And Geordie turned one. And Cummings took to gauging the rising water. Suppose it did reach those boilers and they blew up? "Jee-zooks!" he muttered, and even more feverishly than Dinnie or Geordie took to turning valves till there were no more to turn. He would surely have bolted up the ladder then but for the sight of these two professional stokers still on the job. Just two stokers! And for what? Jee-zooks, for what?

"It 'll be the wather-tight doors now, Geordie," said Dinnie.

"Oh, ay, the water-tight doors, Dinnie."

Cummings saw them wading through the blackened water—away from the ladder. "Say, ain't you people ever coming?" yelled Cummings, and then the electric lights flickered, recovered, flickered, and went out.

"This way, Geordie," he heard Dinnic calling, and heard, too, the heavy swishing of their bodies as they pushed through the water. He could hear, too—must be at the bulkhead now—the directing words to each other, and after a moment the dull thud of a closing door. He could hear, too—

so vehemently were they working and so eager was he for it—he could hear, despite the racket of the outrushing steam, the click of the buttoning keys in the dark.

"And now the injine-room, Geordie."

"Oh, ay, the engine-room doors, Dinnie," and the pair of heavily moving bodies came toward him again. And passed him, and on toward the engine-room. Cummings let his hands drop, and pulled them up hurriedly—they were wet. What—to his hips already? What lobsters, those two! And yet there they were—still on the job. He felt of the ladder to locate it afresh, and then—jee-zooks! —he turned and waded for the engine-room himself.

He could hear Geordie before he reached them. "And that 'ere helectric-light machine flooded and not heven a lantern, Dinnie! A blarsted rotten un I calls this ship."

"Rotten enough, Geordie b'y, but hush now. And did we turn all the keys, I dunno? Wait, if these matches are only dhry." Cummings saw the flare of it and the light held high above Dinnie's head. He saw, too, the two top keys, not yet turned. "Let me," he said—"I'm taller."

"What! and you here yet? Well, well, that's the b'y. Now the other one. That's it. And now for the other dure."

Heroes

"Jee-zooks! Dinnie, but ain't there any end to this? Up to my chest already."

"Hush, b'y, hush! What harm is a little wather on your chest?"

"Won't she sink under us?"

"I dunno will she or no. But she sur-r-tinly will if we don't get that other dure closed—and that soon."

"Ay, an' bloody well soon."

They reached the other door and began on the keys. But they would not turn. "'Tis the bulkhead bucklin' under the weight of the sea. You have the weight, Geordie—throw yourself agin it whilst the two of us turns them. Come, b'y, come now. Now, Geordie! Now agin! There she is. And now agin! That's it. And agin! And now for the way out. Come on, Geordie b'y. And where are you, avick? Where are you, me bowld New Yorker?"

"Here," called out Cummings hastily.

"Wait. Maybe I can light another match to see the way out. I've been kapin' these around me neck with me tobacco to hold 'em dhry like, but I fear—yes, the little divils they're wet. Well, we'll have to find it in the dark. Lay the coorse, b'y, and lay it shtraight. Geordie's no champeen at swimmin' and sorra the shtroke can I swim at all mesel'."

249

"Can't swim—and water to our necks! Well, I can swim all right. Here, take hold of my hand," and with joined hands the three of them made the ladder. They leaned on the hand-rail of the grated hatch to get breath. The sweat was rolling off Cummings, but he was safe and the ship was safe and everybody aboard was safe.

IV

STILL as could be lay the little stowaway while the stokers off watch came into the room and made ready to turn in. Not such a terrible lot, but they did swear; a couple of them more than they ought to, more even than the big Englishman Geordie. He snuggled his head under Dinnie's coat, which was his pillow, and lay quiet, wondering how long the last one, who was sitting on the edge of his bunk smoking, how long before he would roll back into his bunk; and watching him, fell asleep. And sleeping, had a dream, a beautiful dream of being home with his father; and then a terrible dream of the bunk tumbling in and of his father suddenly changing into half a dozen tramping, excited men, and jumping up and running out the door.

The lad sat up, glad to find himself still in his bunk, and yet as he looked he saw the last of his

room-mates running into the passageway. And
a lot of other people were running through the
passageway, past the door, and calling to each
other as they ran. By then he knew that something funny had happened, and he fished out his
shoes from under the bed-tick and put them on
and stepped into the passageway himself, and no
sooner there than a man bowled him over—and
another and another, and two or three more,
every one running swiftly, and only the last of all
stopping to put him on his feet, and even that one
hollered at him, "You bloody little bloater, what
you doin' here? Get up on deck"—roughly, like
that, and yet not unkindly.

The stowaway, finding his feet, started running
himself. All the lights were out—dark everywhere; so that he bumped in and out of passageways and by and by upstairs, slipping by
passengers, and more passengers, like shadows in
the dark, in gangways and on stairways, most of
them excited and asking all sorts of questions,
but mostly, "What's happened?" And then he
reached the top deck, where were a lot of ship's
people hurrying by, but they not saying much.
And he heard the sound of blows and went over to
see what it was, and found a lot of men, one of
them with an axe trying to knock away a big block
of wood from under a life-boat, but not doing it

very well. There were plenty of orders, but nobody seemed to know just what to do. Some said this was the way to do it, and some said no, the other way. And somebody lit a match, and when it blazed up the stowaway saw the buttons shining on the short jackets; and by that he knew them for stewards, and, the stewards being the enemies of Dinnie and Geordie, he slipped in behind the boat.

There he couldn't help hearing the talk. A lot of talk, mostly the talk of men afraid of something. "Wot do hi know of 'andlin' boats?" one was complaining. "*Hi* shipped for a steward, hi did. Where's their bloody s'ilors?"

"Sailors?"—this voice not so frightened. "Sailors on these packets? Sailors? My word, that's a rare one!"

Then a new voice among them. "Over'aul that gear!"

"But 'ow do I hover'aul it?" from the man who said he shipped for a steward, and so close that the stowaway could have reached around the end of the boat and touched his trouser-leg.

"How? Over'aul it, I say!"

"But wot do I do? Hi shipped for a steward an' not for——"

"Clear it away and no more o' your bloody lip!"

Heroes

He felt the steward press close to the boat and then saw his feet leave the deck, as if he was springing up to get hold of something. And then, "Ah-h, hi 'ave it!"

" 'Ave you? Then suppose you do something with it!"

The stowaway could almost feel the legs of the steward stiffen as he braced himself to tug on the rope, and then "Oh-h!—" he heard, and suddenly, almost down on top of him, came the body of the steward. A big block with rope running from it rattled down beside him.

"Gawd!" he heard another voice, and he reached out a hand himself to touch the head of the steward, and it came away wet. The fog and the dew of night lay all about, but it wasn't that. He shivered.

"Gawd's sake!" said the same rough voice, "to think of 'im knowin' no better than that!"

" 'Ow was 'e to know?" came from another. "Fred 'e didn't ship for no s'ilor."

Then came one with a lantern and looked. The stowaway could see it, sidewise—the mashed head and the awful bloody face. He didn't want to look any more. And then another man spotted him and grabbed him. "You bloody little rat, wot you doin' 'ere?" and picked him up and threw him yards across the deck. And he ran off, and the last thing he heard was, " 'E's got 'is larst tip, has Fred."

The stowaway had no idea where he was going, but he ran downstairs and into a passageway, and then down another flight of stairs and into another passageway, and kept on going—away from the terrible dead man.

By and by he found his way among a lot of boxes and barrels, and there hid. And here came some men with a lantern soon and began to haul the boxes and barrels about; and by and by again more men joined them, and then he heard a ripping, like they were breaking some wooden box open, and then he heard, "We might's well have it, same as our betters."

"And was he drinking—on the level, was he?"

"Ay, swillin' it in. I saw 'im myself—in 'is cabin."

"Ay, and so did I," affirmed another. "Before ever we left the dock he was drinkin'. Never misses a chance, he don't. And that tall officer—wot's 'is name?—but, hi say, don't stop to draw no cork," and followed then the crack of a breaking bottle and a deep gurgling.

"Farley, you mean? I 'eard a parsenger myself arsk Farley if 'e 'ad the right time—at the 'ead of the gangplank, mind you, people comin' and goin' all the time—afore we left the dock at all. And Farley, bli' me, 'e couldn't tell 'im, 'is bloomin' heyes a-rollin' in 'is 'ead. Only looks at 'is watch and says, 'Arf-parst seven.' 'E carries Lunnun and New York time on 'is watch, you know, Farley does. 'Ere, let me 'ave a taste now."

More gurgling, and then: "And the parsenger 'e looks at Farley and says, 'Wot?' And Farley looks again and says, 'Yes, 'arf-parst seven,' 'e says again. And the parsenger says, 'D' y' mind if I look myself?' and 'e looks at the watch and c' looks at Farley and 'e says, 'Half-past two— thank you,' and goes over to a lady near the rail and says, 'Well, what d' y' know about that?— so drunk he don't know one hand from the other. A ship's officer and drunk—and it only half an hour to sailing! Fine, isn't it?' Ay, so 'elp me, 'e did. But blarst Farley and the 'ole bloomin' cabin gang! Knock the neck hoff another one and 'urry, for the other ship's standin' by and we'll be 'avin' to go over the side soon."

"Soon? What do you call soon? They won't get the first boat over the side for two hours, by the way they're goin' at it. Know as much about boats, those chaps, as— Well, here's happy days!"

And they drank and went away. And more came, and more, and by and by they began to quarrel, so that the stowaway, terribly frightened, crawled farther in. No light in there. And by and by nobody came any more, and it grew awfully quiet above and outside—no hurrying feet any more. And then he felt around to get out, but found the boxes and barrels were wedged in around him. He tried and tried, but couldn't move them.

So he gave it up at last and lay back, waiting and waiting, until he must have fallen asleep; for the next thing he knew it was darker than ever. And again he tried to get out. But no use. And then he began to feel hungry. But nothing to eat. And then he didn't care if the stewards did come and get him. But they didn't come—nobody came. And then he felt the ship moving under him. And he must have fallen asleep again, for all at once the voices broke in on him and the noise of people throwing the boxes and barrels about. He could not make out just what they were saying, but he felt frightened again and kept quiet till the ship took to rolling, but not rolling like before—a new way now. "She's sinking!" he whimpered, "and I'm locked in here and nobody knows it. And I'll sink with the ship. And be drowned in here!" And "O my father!" he called out then, and "O Dinnie, Dinnie!—O father!"

Heroes

"God in heaven! him in here and not so much as a needle of light to guide us! Where are ye, lad—let another whoop out of ye!" O the blessed voice—Dinnie's voice.

V

THE passengers had been taken off, the ship's company had been taken off, everybody taken off but the two officers on the bridge and themselves —the little fellow hidden—below. It was a night of vaporish fog and sea like oil. From ahead Cummings could hear the chug, chug of the towing tugs. He could not see what they were doing on the bridge, but presently he saw that the towing steamer had cut or slipped her hawser and was headed about. "Jee-zooks! what's that for?" he muttered, and then he heard a revolver shot from the bridge and saw the blue signal flame burning near the rail of the ship. Then he felt the deck under him heave logily and, looking back, saw that her stern was settling. "Jee-zooks! Dinnie had it right—they're going to let her go."

Two more shots rang out and a moment later the second automatic blue light spurted up from the water. One of the towing steamers was now alongside and the two officers were staggering down from the bridge. Cummings ran aft and below, but before he made the next deck he met the two stokers, Dinnie holding the boy in his arms. The water was coming up the iron ladder after them.

"A close call I guess you people had. And a close call yet—hurry!"

"Hurry? What the divil do you think we're doin'—takin' a nap, is it? But is there a boat handy, b'y?"

"There's two of our life-boats alongside. One they'll take, of course. We can take the other. Y' ought to seen them! Talk about a pair of shines! But come on—right after me."

When they reached the open deck her taffrail was all but flush with the water. "Goin' she is, but time enough if the boat's handy."

"Handy enough," assured Cummings, and as they all made their way forward the two stokers looked about. "I call this as comfortable a sink-in', Geordie, as a man could ashk for. Inshore wather, a shmooth sea—on'y for the little b'y. How are ye, lad?"

They heard Cummings's startled voice then.

"What's it? No? Heaven save us, Geordie —the other boat casht adrift! And oh, the little lad!"

"But 'e's over arter her! Look at 'im, Dinnie! Gawd, Dinnie, 'e can swim like a bloody pawpuss."

Heroes

They could hear rather than see him then, kicking through the water. Then he passed out of sight and hearing. A silence, a terribly long silence, during which they saw dimly a ship's life-boat with the two officers shove off from the farther side of the ship. Then they could make out the sound of oars—from their own side of the ship. A minute, two minutes more, perhaps. But now the ship's stern had gone under and her bow mounting.

They began to fear that the New Yorker would never get back in time. "If it was but a loose spar or summat to 'ang on to like, arter she goes under, Dinnie."

"Loose spars? On the deck of an ocean liner? You might lay hold of one of them iron derrick booms. But, thanks to God, Geordie, she'll go down aisy-like."

And it was so. Their ship was six hundred feet long and she could not have been in more than two hundred feet of water, with the result that her stern rested on bottom while her bow was yet high in the air. As her waist went under they climbed up into the forward stays and waited for Cummings.

"A 'eavy boat—'e'll never mike it."

"The tide's agin him—wait a while."

Gently up and down the ship's bow went. Up

and down, up and down, lower and lower. Her forward rail was about under and as yet hardly a ripple on the water.

"Like a bloody submarine," said Geordie, and with a loose line in his hand swarmed up the stays after Dinnie. By now they could see him—faintly. " 'E'll never mike it, Dinnie—'ere goes for 'im."

Geordie hove his coiled line—far out. Her forward rail was all but under. "Hi do believe 'e's got it! 'Ere, tike this end, Dinnie. I've the bight of it. 'Ere goes!"

"God speed ye, Geordie! And I'll soon be afther ye wi' the lad." Already the sea was beginning to walk up the stays. Soon she would go with a rush. Dinnie lifted the boy to his hip and climbed higher.

The line had struck across the gunnel of the lifeboat, whereat Cummings dropped the oars, took hold, and hauled, and in came Geordie—floundering. They heard Dinnie's voice. "To her mashthead 'twill be soon. I'm coming now—wi' the lad—haul hard!" and the splash. The two men hauled. A heavy load it was, and they saw him go under trying to hold the boy clear—once, twice, three times he went, but always kicking vigorously. But they got the pair at last, taking first the little stowaway whom Dinnie handed up.

They got the pair at last, taking first the little stowaway

" 'Tis full of wather I am," he said, and fell
weakly into the bottom of the boat, where he lay
for perhaps a minute before he spoke again.
"Mortal feared I was—where is he, the little lad?
All right, avick? Sure ye are."

Cummings stood up to look about. Not a
sign of their ship; hardly a mark on the water.
"Now for that other towing steamer," he said.
"She's been over to the other steamer and is
headed back. I wonder do they see us. Don't
hail." And they paddled their life-boat close to
the second towing steamer's lights. "The farther
side," whispered Cummings, "and easy." And
on the farther side, with nobody to see, they
climbed aboard. "Turn her adrift, b'y," said
Dinnie, "before she's noticed." Cummings let
the painter slip and the boat drifted off.

They crept along the house and into a passageway, where they came on a man who was gazing
over the rail as if absorbed in some spectacle.
"Jee-zooks!"—Cummings gripped Dinnie—"I'll
bet I know that chap. Hey, there, Tom White!"

The man turned and saw Cummings. "Well,
where in h——"

"Sh-h— We're off that ship, and it mightn't
be healthy for us if some people found it out.
Hide us somewhere, will you, till we get in?"

"Sure. Come on," and led them to a room

with six bunks. "Turn in there and don't hurry to turn out—this bunch will keep their mouths shut. And give me your clothes and I'll dry 'em out below. We'll get you ashore all right. And say, what kind of a team is that up there? What? Really ship's officers? Holy cats! But they sure must 'a' lost their nerve. Says one to the other, coming over the side, 'You were game to the last, Jack,' and puts his arm around his shoulder. What d' y' think o' that, after losin' that grand ship? Didn't they know enough to shore up those weakened bulkheads before putting her under tow, or did they want to lose her? Ought to go to jail either way, the pair of 'em."

"Jail!" said Cummings. "I guess not. That 'd put the company in bad with the public."

"That's right, come to think. But think of 'em, the pair of 'em handin' out that kind of talk! Jee, but I'd like to be around when they tell their story ashore. Game to the last! Holy cats, but what a couple of shines!"

VI

The three stokers and the boy, having reached New York, were now viewing the steamship office from the Broadway sidewalk. Dinnie and Geordie were for holding back, but not Cummings.

Heroes

"What y' afraid of—that buttoned nigger at the door? Or the fat furniture inside? Come on in and get your money."

Cummings led the way in, and claimed for all three, and was told to come back in an hour. Geordie and Dinnie, overawed by the superior air of everybody, were for doing as they were told; but "Go out and come back hell!" retorted Cummings. "We want the wages due us. We can't be waiting around all day. We've had no breakfast and we've no money for dinner, and we want our wages—the wages due us," and made such a further fuss over it that the clerk went inside and brought out a well-cushioned, florid man with blue-black cheeks and curled-up mustache, which he continued to curl. He was dressed in one of the company's uniforms.

"I knows 'im," whispered Geordie. " 'E's the purser."

"Now, m' lads," began the purser.

"M' lads hell!" snapped Cummings. "Don't m' lad us. We're all tired out and—hungry—and we want our wages."

On the purser's too-closely shaven features a pitying expression would have crept, but Cummings's sardonic grin cracked it midway. "Very well, I'll see," said the purser. "You know how much is due you, of course?"

"No, we don't."

"Well, there's three days coming to you."

"Three days hell! We shipped for the voyage."

At this point the purser backed away and another official hove into view. A much keener chap this than any purser. He restated the case for them. "You shipped for the cruise—exactly. But you did not, it appears, complete the voyage. You left 'ere on the twenty-third and your ship went down on the twenty-fifth. Twenty-three, twenty-four, twenty-five, which makes three days due you, at four p'und ten a month."

"But, look 'ere—" Geordie was gathering indignation to himself.

"No looking here or there," retorted this keen one. "Look at the law. The law says that when a ship goes down all claims against her cease. That's maritime law."

Cummings was taken aback. But this was no blustering, self-important man, he felt. This one knew his ground, evidently. He felt like punching somebody. "Well"—he turned to his chums—"they got us, I guess. Here you, give us those three days."

They got their money. Cummings, looking at his, began to figure mentally. "Four pound ten —that's twenty-two dollars about—three-thirty-firsts of twenty-two. Jee-zooks!"

Heroes

Geordie held his in one open palm. "Bli' me, but it's 'ardly eight bob!"

"Glory be!" said Dinnie softly, "but wouldn't you think they'd pay us to the end of the month itsel'? Wouldn't you?" and just then was a great commotion and in the rush they were pushed to one side. "What the divil's all the ballyhooin' about?" asked Dinnie. They were at the door in time to see an automobile rumbling up.

"Jee-zooks!" ejaculated Cummings. "Look—our two officers!"

The cheering crowd was surging up the steamship company's steps. The three stokers and the boy had difficulty in holding their feet and their places on the sidewalk. A newsboy was yelling in Cummings's ear.

"What's that?" ejaculated Cummings.

"Sure—here's all about them," said the boy, and spread the first page of the paper out. Cummings took it in—the black letters four inches high.

"Well, what d' y' think o' that?"—

HEROIC CONDUCT OF CAPTAIN HADSBY—
MODERN SEA HISTORY KNOWS
NO PARALLEL.

Cummings looked his paper over quickly. He bought another and looked that over, and another. "That's right, fellows—they've all got the same thing," and began to read the story. It took a whole page to tell it—of the dauntless two who refused to leave their ship till the last bit of her went under the sea—would have gone down with her—did go down into the seething maelstrom, but by a miracle——

"Hi s'y, lad, that's not in any piper?"

"Just as I'm reading it."

"Hand 'oo told that to these 'ere pipers?"

"Why, he did."

" 'E did? 'oo did?'

"The captain, our captain, himself."

"Lave me see the paper, b'y." Dinnie had a look for himself. "An' he towld these reporthers that? But it must be a mishtake. Sure, even if it was thrue he wouldn't say it—not of himsel', b'y, not of himsel'."

"But he did. Listen. *'As the last bit of her fore-truck sank beneath the seething, boiling sea* '"

"Seethin'! B'ilin'! God forgive him!"

"—*'he dived and secured a floating spar*——'"

"A floating spar? Ho, ho, that's a rare un! Where'd the bloody floating spar come from?"

"Loose spars on the deck of an ocean liner— 'tis kind of a cute notion. If he would but shtick to nathure itsel'!"

"No matter, he's getting away with it." Cummings scowled at the paper and then he looked at Geordie, and from Geordie to Dinnie. He looked over the palpitating, still cheering crowd, and laughed—hysterically. "Jee-zooks! I can't help it—it's the limit."

"Gawd!" uttered Geordie—"a 'ero!"

"What kind are they at all?" asked Dinnie, "these reporthers he towld this to?"

"Why, they're the slickest on earth, let them tell it. Yes, sir, the slickest—and every damn one of 'em's fallen for that Belasco back-drop with all the calciums full-tilt and our heroic captain in the middle of every spot-light."

"Hi!" said Geordie, " 'ere they come again, the bloomin' 'eroes!"

They were coming down the steps and the crowd was cheering anew. "Three cheers and a tiger for Captain Hadsby!" called out somebody. They were given, and Captain Hadsby raised his hat and bowed—and smiled. "Three cheers for his brave mate!" and the crowd cheered again, and Farley bowed—and smiled. "Jee-zooks, pipe that smile!" muttered Cummings.

"There's the kind of seamen I'd like to see on the bridge of any ship I cross in," came one voice from the crowd. Cummings turned and saw him—an honest citizen gazing admiringly. "You would, eh?" snapped Cummings. "Well, you're a hell of a fine judge of seamen!"

Heroes

The automobile had difficulty in getting away, so dense was the crowd; but the slow start gave the admiring throng a chance to cheer again, whereat the brave Captain Hadsby lifted his hat and bowed again, and his equally brave subordinate did likewise.

Geordie was gazing after them open-mouthed. "Well, wot d' y' s'y to that! My Gawd!" and suddenly shook his fist passionately after them. "'Eroes! Yes, you're a bloody fine 'ero now, but wite till the Board o' Tride across the water gets arter you. Then we'll see if you're a 'ero or no. 'Eroes! I s'y, lad, look 'ere. If the likes o' them be 'eroes, then wot of us—of Dinnie and me and you that saved all the ship's parsengers —wot about us?"

"Us?" Cummings bit it out. "Us? Why, we're a bunch of cheap pikers. We're three slobs of stokers at four pound ten a month—and our wages stops the minute our ship goes down."

The automobile was still in plain view proceeding up Broadway, not going so fast, however, but what the populace was given a chance to identify the valiant mariners and to cheer them afresh.

Cummings gazed and swore. Geordie gazed and cursed.

Dinnie only shook his head sadly. Then: "Come on, b'y. Come on, Geordie—don't be

Heroes

mindin' them. They're like those stewards we were spakin' about the other mornin'. 'Tis part of their work for the company. Surely in their hearts they must be havin' the black thoughts o' themselves. And for all the praise they do be gettin' from foolish people, you b'y, and Geordie, and me, we're no worse off. We—we're still men before God." He stooped and patted the little boy's cheek. "Sure it's here's the one had the har-r-d, har-r-d time of it, wasn't it, avick? Sure it was, yes. And we have yet to get you home. Come on, Geordie; come on, b'y—it's time we were hunting another ship."

The crowds were still cheering, one batch after another, as the automobile moved on. Cummings turned for a last look. He held his half-smoked cigarette in his peculiar fashion, high in the air between thumb and second finger. Still the cheers were coming from the distance and Cummings was listening. "Heroes! Heroes!" he bit out, and snapped the cigarette butt half-way across the street. "Heroes!—jee-e-z'ks—heroes!" and hurried after his chums.

THE CHRISTMAS HANDICAP

The Christmas Handicap

THE race in which I defeated the so-called Australian for the championship of America was worth two thousand dollars to me, which two thousand, barring a few inevitable dollars spent in treating the crowd, I should have brought home to my wife and little girl, and so made sure that all would be well with them till the next season. And so I intended, but in the most accidental way in the world we—Fifield, the book-maker, was with me—we ran into a faro-bank on the way home, and in the morning I came away with about enough to pay for a good breakfast at a hotel, for after that I would not go home. I had said on leaving my wife that I would come back to her with the money in my pocket or not at all.

I had to borrow a half-dollar off Fifield to tip the waiter. "Tell my wife I've gone, but don't tell her where," I said to Fifield, and went on down to the docks and shipped on a cattle-steamer. Not what you might call one of the preferred occupations, feeding cattle and cleaning their stalls, but not laborious, either. Only

273

the food—the men's food—is not what it might be, even for men down on their luck. And the men are not always what they might be. Plenty of good-enough people, some who are unfortunate or some just adventurous ones among them, but sometimes also a bad one. There was one who did not take to me any more than I took to him, a big brute of a chap, the heavy-weight bully of the after-hold. Perhaps he thought I was as meek as I must have seemed blue—he must have thought so, for nothing in my build or looks should have led him to think I could not put up a fight with anything walking God's earth. The afternoon I ran the Australian, I had stripped at one hundred and eighty-two pounds, and not a pound of it you could have torn off with anything less than a cotton-hook. And make no mistake, I was still in condition; one night at the gaming-table, nor four days of bad food on the steamer, was not pushing me back to the second class.

This chap picked a fight with me, and I threw him into a stall where four Colorado steers would have trampled him to death had not his mates hauled him out onto the alley-way in a hurry. "And if we'd been on deck I'd just as soon 've thrown you overboard—and could do it as easy as I say it, too," I ripped out at him, and so I would, or to any man who came at me as he had.

The Christmas Handicap

Once I got warmed up I did not mind taking a chance at 'most anything. I had backed the starter's gun in too many big races not to have nerve, and had carried my weight down the track at too fast a clip too many times not to know I had power.

But if this chap was a surprised man, he was not altogether giving up the fight; at least he was believed to be the man who, a few nights later, dropped a bale of hay down the hold onto me, who was stretched out on the hatch two decks below. Sometimes those bunks on cattle-ships are not any too clean, and I was sleeping out this night. Now a bale of hay falling through the height of two decks doesn't come down like any hatful of feathers. It loosened two of my ribs, so said the head-steward, who had once studied medicine and was the nearest thing to a doctor the ship carried, and who, after a fashion, also trussed me up. He did not make a good job of the bandaging—even he himself said as much—which probably caused him also to say: "But what can you expect? The man ought to be dead, anyway!" But I wasn't, though when the inflammation set in and the fever began to keep me awake nights I almost wished I was. Almost, but not quite— there was always the wife and the child in mind.

In Liverpool, after the ship was docked, I collected what money was coming to me for the eleven days' passage. But first I beat up the man who probably dropped the bale of hay on me, beat him up good in a quiet out-of-the-way alley in a part of Liverpool where cattle-men and their kind hang about. There are regions there where the police take scant notice when two of the guild engage in battle, provided it does not become too general, or they do not take to welting too many outsiders.

They probably aim not to debauch their help, those steamship lines—ten shillings was coming to me for the trip. Some of the crew said I was lucky not to be docked a few bob for the three days I was laid up with the floating ribs. And doubtless so, but from out of that two dollars and a half I bought a third-class ticket to Manchester, where I remembered was a man famous in America for backing professional sprint-runners. I found his place—a "pub" with a sort of eating-house attached. There I ordered my roast-beef and potatoes and a mug of ale, and they did taste nourishing. As I ate and drank I gave ear to the talk going on around me. It was all of horses, whippets, and foot-running. I soon learned what I most wanted to know—before New Year's there would be several good professional handicaps, with the betting on them promising to be lively.

The Christmas Handicap

Before I had finished my meal the master himself came in and sat down among his customers. I took a good look at him. A pretty decent sort he appeared, one who might have the nerve to take a chance on a man who could show him a good performance, and who might give a fellow a fair share of the winnings after he had won; which coincided with what I had heard of him. A square "gaffer," the professional sprinters termed him.

After I had smoked my single pipeful, which I allowed myself after every meal when not in strict training, I picked up my little bag, which held my running clothes and shoes, a pair of running corks, a tooth-brush, and a hair comb— nothing more—and approached my man. "Mr. Ensey, I've been doing a bit of sprinting on the other side. It's no use telling what I'm good for —you'll have a chance to see that for yourself if you'll take me on. Will you bed and board me till I've had a fair try-out?" I said no more than that then.

The old fellow looked me over. He would probably have looked a horse over in pretty much the same way except that he paid more attention, possibly, to my face than he might if I were a horse. "What do you weigh?" he asked at last.

The Christmas Handicap

"I did strip at one hundred and eighty-two pounds two weeks ago."

"M—m—thirteen stone. But you don't weigh that now?"

"No—o—probably not."

"And why?"

I might have told him of the broken ribs and the fever, but I did not care to. It sounded too much like an excuse. I have small use myself for men who are always producing excuses, good-sounding excuses though they be, in place of performances. This man was concerned in my running, not in my troubles. How fast could I swing through a hundred and fifty yards, not how did I happen to get a couple of cracked ribs, was what the old gaffer wanted to know. So now I answered, "It must have been the bad passage."

"H—m— My lad, if you lose nigh a stone-weight crossing the Atlantic, I'm not sure you've the timber to stand the hard training we put a handicap runner through here. But what 've you ever done on the other side?"

I hesitated to answer, but finally did say: "I've done evens," meaning ten seconds for a hundred yards.

He smiled ever so little. "H—m— Not too many 'ave showed me evens over here—not for *my* watch. Them ten-second amachurs can't ever

278

show better than a quarter or 'alf second for me."

"I'm no amateur."

"Well, on another look, I'll give you credit, I don't think you are. I'm puttin' you down for something better than a cup-huntin' amachur. But what's your name? I must 've heard of you if you're anything great."

I wanted to be honest with him—I liked the old fellow already—but I preferred not to give my name just then. "Suppose you let that go for awhile?"

"H—m—m. Well, please yourself, but when a man's goin' to the expense of taking care of you for some weeks maybe he's not askin' o'ermuch to know your name. But please yourself. I like your looks."

That same afternoon I ran a trial for him. The blue feeling was on me again, and my side aching terribly. I knew I could not run fast enough to get away from a policeman, but I went with Ensey to the track. A dozen or more idlers, curious to see the American run, also went along.

I did my best, but I had to run alone—and I never could run well alone, though I did not tell the gaffer so. As I say—excuses are no recommendation to a man who is risking money on you.

The Christmas Handicap

After I had crossed the finish line I allowed my momentum to carry me, in the customary way, on for fifty yards or so, so as not to strain anything by stopping too suddenly. By the time I had returned to the old man he had replaced the watch in his pocket and I did not ask to look at it. But it was very slow I knew. The faces of the idlers, not to mention their comment, proved that. "Huh—that chap. 'E can't run as fast as my old woman," says one. That was enough.

I was in the dressing-room, about to get out of my running togs, when the gaffer entered. "Eh, lad, how long is it since you've run in ten seconds on the other side?"

"Oh—not so long."

"M—m—but you do fall away fast. What d' y' think you did to-day?"

I said I had no idea. I dreaded to be told; and the old fellow guessed as much. "And I don't know as I blame you, lad. It was—" He whispered it, as he might some shameful secret.

Well, I could believe it, though not since my first race in public, one for boys of sixteen years, had I run so slow.

"And the marvel is you've such a grand style. I do like your style, lad."

"Well—" I was lying on the rubbing-board, the pain of my side forced me to lie down. "I suppose you won't care to keep me after that trial."

"I didn't say that, lad, though on the judgment of it I shouldn't be wasting another ha'penny on you. But I can't get over your style. You've got the style of a champion—you have that—and I must say, too, every other mark of a champion but the speed. What is it—what's wrong?"

I had got as far as removing my spiked shoes in the undressing process when the gaffer had entered, and there I stopped. I wanted him to think that his entrance had put out of my mind the thought of further undressing. I wanted him to leave before I pulled off my running shirt; but plainly he was going in no hurry. And the longer I delayed the more bound he was to stay. At length I could not help seeing that he was suspicious of something or other. Well, the truth was better than some sorts of suspicion, and, after all, if he was ever to back me why shouldn't he know? I drew off my shirt, and then old Ensey saw the bandage about my body.

"Eh, lad—what's that 'ere?"

Then I told him, and how I came by it.

"And was it right, d' y' think, to hide it from me—me that's to be put to the expense of keeping ye?" But he was mostly sympathy. "And ye tried to run with that? Man, it's resting, not running, ye should be. Come, now, and lay by a week or two, and then we'll see what ye'll make of it."

I rested two weeks, jogged easily for another week, and then showed a gain of six yards over that first trial. "Ah—h—that's more like, but a long ways off yet of championship form." I did not tell him that once out of my running I was rather slow to come around, nor that my weakness was not yet gone; nor that raw, foggy weather, as they had this day, was terribly discouraging. Dry weather always for me. Cold or hot, no matter, so it be dry.

Another week and I ran two yards faster. Four days later another yard came off. "You surely are coming, lad. Show me a quarter second off that again and I'll give you a pair of pumps—" (spiked shoes he meant) "off the best shoemaker in England."

"You can order them for next week," I answered to that. And on the day appointed I won my pumps; and that same day I was entered for the next handicap. I was not so far short of my true form then, for it must be remembered that in all my trials I had run alone. And, as I have said, running alone never suited me. I needed some-body alongside trying to pass me, or somebody ahead striving to beat me out. To me any race at all meant two yards above my practice time. A big race, with a great crowd, and, it might be, a band of music, with the cheering and shouting, the betting calls and so on—a championship, or match for big money—meant from three to four yards to me. I never could run cold. I suppose it was that my imagination as well as muscle had to be tuned up before I could get all that was in me out.

But I said nothing of all this to my gaffer, and a week later when I won my handicap, showing form equal to ten seconds flat, the old man was taken by surprise.

"Ay, lad, but if I'd a notion ye were that kind I'd made a pot of money on ye—twenty-five to one against. I'd only five pounds down on ye. Why, you're a real racer. And you're in rare form." And he really thought so; but I was not yet in form. I had told Ensey that I had done ten seconds in America. As a matter of fact the day I won from the Australian I had done nine and four-fifths seconds, though the time was returned as ten seconds; and at that, after going fifty yards, certain I could not lose, I had let down. And further, though this was known to but a few good friends, I had done inside nine and three-fifths seconds in a race before that. On that occasion, also, the watches had caught me in ten seconds, which was correct, but the course was five yards over the hundred—a mistake that did no harm. I was after a living, not records. But what use *telling* the gaffer what I could do when there would soon be a chance to *show* what I could do?

Of the thirty pounds I received for winning that first race I sent Fifield twenty for my wife and little one, but saying also that he must not tell her where I was; otherwise she would be over on the next steamer, which was not what I wanted. Too many people here that I did not want her to mix with, and also I did not want to face her until I had made good that two thousand dollars. The balance, ten pounds, I handed back to my gaffer, saying, "Just before we go to the post in the next race lay that on me," which, when the time came, the gaffer did, at ten to one.

But now they had discovered who I was, and classed me accordingly, on my reputed speed, nine and four-fifths seconds for the hundred. I would hereafter be back-mark man, on scratch with the English champion, whom I had not yet met. I won that race, one hundred and thirty yards, in twelve and two-fifths seconds, and that for the jealous watches of men whose living depended on their getting it to half a yard.

The old gaffer, for whom I was gladder than for myself, hugged me in his joy. "Lad, lad, but ye do storm at the finish. I never see aught like the way ye came through that last thirty yards. Where'd ye learn it?"

I did not tell him that I could have come yet faster if it were needed, but—"You'll enter me for the big Christmas 'cap now," I did say.

"That I will, and if your mark isn't too restrictive, I'll lay more than a few pounds on ye."

"Oh, no fear but I'll be well back on an impossible mark this next time. They'll not have the American running away with any more 'caps for awhile again."

How he chuckled at that! "You have it right! You've done what no stranger ever did before— win two 'caps. And I'm proud enough to have had the 'andling of you. Ay, they'll make it impossible for ye next time, but ye'll try for a place if naught else? Ay, that's it. And there's no doubt ye'll meet our English champion—they say he's saving himself for it. How do you like the notion of meeting him?"

"It suits me. But I'll want a special preparation for it, the same as he'll get."

"You'll have it, lad, as good a preparation as any sprinter in England ever 'ad—as 'Arry 'Utchins 'imself ever 'ad. And we'll put you in a stable at Sheffield to train for it."

The Christmas Handicap

II

IT is in England, where stables of professional runners are kept as if they were stables of horses, that they know how to get a sprinter in shape. During my eight weeks' preparation I slept, with four others, in a large back ell-room of a small hotel in Sheffield. Every night at ten we were locked in that room by a little old, scrappy Scotchman, who kept the keys in his pocket and slept on the other side of the door. Every morning at half-past six we were called for a stroll, to take the kinks out of legs and back and arms and to put the fresh air into our lungs. Returning from that we were towelled lightly, then allowed to sit down to breakfast. At ten or half-past we dropped down to the grounds for practice. No hard working—just a fooling around and a few starts, but finishing up with a long, easy swinging quarter in fifty-five or fifty-six seconds, to start the sweat. In the afternoon we did our fast work. After each practice we were given a good rub-down; and before turning in at night we were rubbed down again.

We were worked like race-horses, fed like horses, with the best of food and plenty of it—this little hotel was famous for its good beef and chops and vegetables—and at night we slept like horses. The five of us, we would tick off to sleep like so many clocks, as Angus used to say. But with all that never a touch of drudgery. It was the work we were best fitted for, the work that of all else on earth we would rather do. Out of sheer love of the game we would have gone through it for nothing; would have paid for the chance, some of us, if not allowed to do it otherwise. And I may say I never knew a world-beater in athletics who did not go at his work with that same feeling. If it were not so he would never have become a champion. And I imagine that it is pretty much that way in any profession.

This work into which we put so much passionate energy was fast bringing us to as near physical perfection as man may get. I know that after six weeks of it, on top of the six weeks of good living that had preceded, I was like a tiger. Cloistered almost, like so many monks, only worse off than monks—no spiritual devotions to counter-balance, with no outlet for our boiling energy but our sprinting practice, our trouble was to hold ourselves in. Returning from the grounds after practice we used, out of excess of animal spirits, to dare each other to all kinds of foolish stunts, may-be betting sixpence or a shilling a corner on the outcome. One afternoon I took in a running

The Christmas Handicap

leap a street that, so they told me, the champion long jumper of middle England had refused to attempt for a hundred pounds. The leap was not extraordinary—nor had I ever trained specially for jumping—a good jump, no more—but the run to it was most uneven and the curbing on which I landed broken and jagged. The thing was that if I did not take off and land just right I would probably break or strain something—my ankle or instep. There were that and other things which I had no notion of attempting until suddenly I found myself doing them. There was the spiked iron fence which surrounded our hotel to the height of a man's shoulder. They dared me, one day, to stand off ten yards from it, hop up to it, then hop over it, in ordinary street clothes and shoes of course, from the brick sidewalk. If I did not clear it, the spikes would probably be driven into my left side or thigh, and I be left in a bad way.

I tackled it and I remember the bar-maid—she was looking through the window of the hotel, a score or more were gathered outside—the bar-maid shrieking as I rose in the air. But she needn't have—I cleared it handily.

But the gaffer got after her when it was all over. He came along too late to stop it. "Don't ever you yell like that again, Miss Arnold, when a man's trying a thing like that. If you can't bear it, don't look." He spoke roughly enough, as he could at times.

"But, Mr. Ensey, who'd ever think he was really going to try it—such an awful thing, and fancy if he slipped up!"

"A wonder he didn't—at your murder yell!"

"But a man don't slip up, Guv'nor, when he's *got* to do a thing," I put in here, wanting to help her out.

"Some don't, maybe. I don't fancy you've eyes or ears for anything but what you're after at the moment, but all men aren't that way. And, Ned, you want to begin to put the brake on. You've got so much bloody energy tearin' round in you now that you'll go crazy or explode soon if you don't watch out. A little will-power is what you need now, lad."

I answered nothing to that, only called for the half-pint of bitter beer which I allowed myself before dinner and supper when in training.

But my gaffer hadn't done yet. He turned to my stable-mates: "Let me ketch any o' you darin' 'im again—just let me! Don't you know 'is temper by this time?—and the trial 'eats less than a week away!"

Going out the door, I looked back to see how they were taking it, and in so doing met the bar-maid's eye. She had her handkerchief to one side of her face as if brushing her flushed cheek, but on the side away from the old man was an expression that I did not know what to make of.

The trial heats of the big handicap, to which my gaffer referred, were run on the second day before Christmas. Being the important running race of the year, a great crowd was present; and by this time there was so much curiosity to see me, the only foreigner who had ever come to England and won two handicaps, that the management offered me fifty pounds to insure my appearance. so I was now, in the eyes of the public, next best man to Rowden, their champion, although the betting men, who are better judges, rated me as his equal; some privately said I was a shade faster. I knew myself I was faster—"a good bit faster," my gaffer said, but not in public.

Rowden and I had the same mark—that is, we both started from scratch; and we both won our first trial heats. There would be great running, everybody said, when we came together. But we never came together. In the semi-finals, an entry that nobody had figured on, a man named Heddon, with nine yards start, stayed so far in the lead that forty yards from home Rowden dropped his arms and gave it up. It was a scandalous beating, and with the report of Heddon's easy win, away flew my chances.

The Christmas Handicap

Leaving the grounds that afternoon, everybody was saying, "Heddon, Heddon? *Who* is this Heddon?"

But trust our shrewd old gaffer to get hold of something about him. He came to me at supper in the hotel. "We're hooked," he began. "I knew him when he used to run in Caledonian outings and small 'caps in Scotland two or three years back, and then he dropped out of sight. His entry would come in from time to time to this handicap and that, but he'd never run. Now we see why he's been running under cover, all this time—only the Lord knows where or under what name. A proper sleeper he is. Laid by till all was right for the killin'. A pot of money for him to win the final, as of course he will. His backer will see that he don't go wrong for that."

"Who's his backer?"

"H—m—m—there now. I've my suspicions, but I'll find out more about it. I've scouts out. I'll be back, by and by, and report."

I finished my supper and smoked my half-pipeful, and then Angus went out for a stroll, to see if he couldn't discover something about Heddon. He invited me to go along, but I said I didn't care to go. "But leave me the keys," I called out after him.

"Oh, ay—" he tossed them back—"the old

guv'nor could always trust you—you're not like the others."

I wanted to be alone, and started for the room, which this night I was to have to myself, because my stable-mates, who had not so much as won a single heat among them all, were through with training. They were now out and about the city enjoying themselves. And how they could and would enjoy themselves! After a man has been exercising like a race-horse and living like an anchorite for months—he is the man who has the capacity for pleasure, not the man who is pursuing it all the time. And pleasure? I slammed my bare hand against the hall wall as I thought of it. It was blessed little pleasure I was having these days. I must have exclaimed aloud at the thought, for a voice said, "Don't take it so to heart."

It was the blonde bar-maid; and if I haven't said much of her before this, don't imagine that she wasn't a factor in the life of the place, or that the light of her beauty was hid under any bushel. And she could measure a man up—the physical and emotional make-up of a man at any rate— as quickly as any old gaffer in the world.

She was the one feature of the hotel which my gaffer did not like. He wanted no women around when men were training. And this was a "specially damn dangerous creature," he used to say, "to be standin' about." All I had to do with her was when I would go in after practice every morning and afternoon and get my half-pint of bitter beer. There, of course, she was always, and naturally I said "Good-morning" or "Good-afternoon" to her.

No every-day bar-maid; with her figure and locks, she would have made a hit on any stage. Our fellows used to put an extra edge on their appetite before meals arguing why she did not go on the stage. "Why don't she?" the old gaffer would answer. "Why? You know damn well why. It's *men*, not Johnnies, she wants."

Whatever the reason, be sure it was not because she could not if she wanted to. I was rather surprised to see her now. She should have been behind the bar. But there she was at the foot of the stairs. She had never been free in her speech with me as with the others; nor was she over-free now. Indeed, there was even a backwardness in her manner.

"You're looking blue," she said. She did not call me by name. She used to call all the others by their Christian names—Joey, or Charlie, or Georgie—but she never addressed me by any name at all, and unless she caught my eye or there was no other person present, she never spoke to me at all. "You're looking blue," she said now.

"I'm *feeling* blue," I said.

"No wonder. But cheer up—no disgrace even if you can't win to-morrow."

"It's not the race!"

"No?"

"No." And looking at her, I thought of another woman. Her face flushed. One hand crept up to her neck-piece. God forgive me for anything in my eyes that made her blush, but 'twas not her just then—'twas a sweeter girl I had in mind.

I went up the stairs. On the landing I looked back. She was still standing there, a handsome woman. She smiled, and going through the door which led to the back of the bar, she smiled again. And there was more than pure kindness in the smile.

I continued to my room. I *was* blue. When you haven't seen or heard from your wife for four months, when you have had no answer to half a dozen letters, when you have been sending money-orders home and no word of acknowledgment of them either, when you know yourself to be a man who never understood women, and there was I only a professional sprinter, when she might have married other men, with any of whom she'd be running no risk of ever wanting for the good things of life—I tell you I *was* blue. And there was the little girl, too.

Well, I had only myself to blame. I had gone off, after throwing away the money won in the big race, without a word, though of course Fifield would explain something of that; would possibly make her understand that it was my old besetting sin, the love of a wager, and not the cold intention, which started me: no close friend of mine, Fifield, but surely friend enough to do that. He had won many a dollar on me—he owed me that little kindness.

There I sat and thought. Nobody came near me. I thought of Angus, probably having a mug of ale somewhere; of the old gaffer, ferreting out news of Heddon. But always my mind would go back to my wife. Why hadn't she sent word? Fifield, too, was to write after he had delivered my message to her; but from him never a word, either.

I was still sitting there when ten o'clock struck. I opened the window, which looked out on the side street. A fine night; many people on the street, and from the "pub" below, which opened also onto the side street, the noise of cheerful voices. Two or three of them plainly were celebrating—had doubtless won a few pounds on the race, won it off men like myself, and they could

The Christmas Handicap

afford to take a drink. *Could* and *would*. But I mustn't. Not me—I was in training. To-morrow night, now, I would be free and could drink - if I cared to—but not to-night. A fine freedom, indeed! A fine life altogether! Putting enough physical and mental energy into my work to bring success to half a dozen tradesmen, and what was I getting out of it? To-morrow I was slated for defeat—a bad defeat. Four yards he might head me. A fine return for weeks of self-denial and effort! Fine, fine! Well, thank the Lord, to-morrow night would end my running.

To-morrow night? Surely I was a proper fool —to-morrow night. Even if I got second place, what was fifty pounds—my gaffer's share? It surely couldn't break him. To sweep up a field of bets was his game. And the next day after was Christmas. A fine Christmas! A merry Christmas! Hadn't seen wife or child in four months, and nigh four thousand miles from home.

About then, or, it may have been an hour later —Lord knows how your mind works at such times—I heard from the yard, which was in the rear of the house, the voice of the room-boy. Whereat I ran—my mind always did get a jumping start—I ran to the rear window and whistled. He answered.

"Come up the back steps," I called.

The Christmas Handicap

He came by way of the back door. I drew out some change. "Bring me up some ale—three bottles. Say nothing to nobody, and bring them up the back way."

He would have brought three bottles of poison just as quickly. In no time he was back.

"Now bring me more—a dozen this time." He went. He was proud to go for me. Wasn't I the fastest sprinter in the world? And wasn't my name, in letters two feet high, adorning every dead wall in town? And my full-length picture in every sporting paper of that week?

He was hardly out of the door when I opened a bottle and gulped it down; and another, and was opening the third when he returned with the twelve bottles, which he set at my feet on the floor, and then handed me a sealed envelope.

"What's this?"

"A note."

"So I suppose. But who from?"

"Oh—h," he leered at me knowingly, cunningly, "you know."

"I know?" I looked at him. He was a precocious one, acquainted with many things before his time. "I know—hah?" I drew the cork out of the third bottle—and slowly let it pour down my throat. "I know—hah? And what is it I know? And how do *you* know I know?"

The Christmas Handicap

"She said you'd know."

"*She?* And whoever *she* is, how did she know you were coming up here?"

"She guessed where I was going—wormed it out of me—I didn't mean to tell, but you can't keep a thing from her. And——"

The door was heard opening below—the front door. And closing. "Sh—sh—it's your gaffer —he's no love for me—but she said she'd be off at twelve," and was gone down the back stairs. Waiting a moment to make sure it was my gaffer's step on the stairs, I pushed the bottles, empty and full, under the bed, and drew down the blanket so that all were hid. The note I stuck in my pocket.

It was the gaffer. He took a seat, pulled out his pipe and then put it back. "Excuse me, Ned, I forgot—for the moment I was fancyin' the running was over."

"And isn't it as good as over?"

"Well, m—m—yes—though you're a man that's likely to do anything in a pinch. I've great faith in you, Ned."

I knew something of my old gaffer's weakness by this time. Any friend of his was a fine fellow, so I passed that over.

He was now regarding me affectionately. "But what's wrong with you? You're not yourself at all. Come, come, Ned—we mustn't let it take such a hold of you. Hold out a while longer—maybe I'll have good news for you in the mornin'."

My mind at the word "news" was far away again.

"Good news of what?"

"Oh—h—I've been doing some investigatin'. And a man whose description fits your gambling friend Fifield, that you told me about, is here and doin' business, though not under that name." Long before this I had told the old gaffer of the race with the Australian and the after-loss of the two thousand dollars.

"But did you see this Heddon run to-day, Ned?"

"No, I was being rubbed when he won that heat from Rowden."

"Well, take a light-haired man of five feet ten, thick-set, heavy calves, specially long in the back, a quick starter, high knee and strong arm action—who would that remind you of?"

It did not come to me till then—yet I was hardly surprised. Perhaps I was too loggy with ale to be much surprised. Perhaps so. "That would fit the Australian who ran me for the American championship."

"Well, that's 'im—but no Australian. That's Heddon—and your friend Fifield's got him under lock and key at the Swan. I must say they planned it well—and stand to get a pot of money—and a good bit o' mine and yours they'll get at the same time. 'Tis Fifield will get most of it, too. He was in drink to-night, and said a lot. He's no love for you."

"And why not—did he say?"

"H—m—m—hints, hints. But suppose 'twas him was behind Heddon when you beat him in America? And suppose—suppose then, Ned—suppose he's in love with your wife?"

"He *was*—wanted to marry her—but he's got over that."

"How d' y' know he's got over it? Suppose he figured he could keep you over here with not money enough to go back home, and she over there with not money enough to buy herself and the little girl bread! How then?"

"You surely do imagine things, Guv'nor."

"Maybe so—maybe so. And maybe I'm only imaginin' he led you into that gamblin' joint where you lost your two thousand! But you're tired, lad. You're up too late as it is—after eleven o'clock—go to bed. And lock that back door. However came it open, anyway? I told Angus never to leave it open. If I see him anywhere I'll send him up to keep you company. You'll make what you can of it, to-morrow, won't you, Ned? —and then a fine lay-off. And mind"—no moaning over the good thing that was being snatched from us, but a fine, warm smile from the old fellow—"mind, I may have great news for you to-morrow. Good-night, Ned."

Great news? Heddon disbarred? No, they could not do that. His running under another name abroad could be no cause for disqualification, even if we cared to play that game, which we had no mind to. They would have to let him run now—and all bets would go at the post—and we would take our medicine.

My head ached. What was the old man's notion of Fifield trying to keep me from my wife? Queer things came into the gaffer's head—the most suspicious man at times.

I leaned out of the rear window. I could hear the voice of the bar-maid whenever she went into the kitchen. Also I could see her shadow against the white fence in the yard. Presently I could hear the old gaffer's voice below. A few minutes and I heard him say "Good-night," and, a moment later, his steady old step going up the side street.

Good old gaffer! Poor old Ned King! Ned King, you poor slob! I drew the blanket up from the floor, reached under the bed, and held a bottle up to the light.

I had a thought that the sight of the ale would

The Christmas Handicap

make me forget my backer. But it did not—not quite. "I told 'em all I didn't care if 'e 'ad twenty-nine instead of nine yards—when Ned King gets after him those nine yards will shrivel up like thin-cut bacon on a hot grill—" I could see him in the bar of the Swan defying all who might care to contradict.

Good old gaffer. And he trusted me. And he had given me a chance; bedded and boarded me when I was down and out. And once again his money was down on me.

Ay, his money was down on me. I counted the full bottles idly. Twelve, and three gone. What a forgetful time I could have yet! And plenty more downstairs. I, who had never until to-night taken the second bottle of ale at one sitting, to-night was going to see how much a man would need to take to make a man forget.

I sat on the edge of my cot. I took pleasure in counting the bottles once more. What a time! To be sure I could. But would I? Would I now? "I says to 'em all before the bar of the Swan—not if 'e 'ad twenty-nine yards! And when Ned King gets after 'im—" Game old gaffer!

Surely I could. I drew the cork of one. The froth welled slowly up. I watched it a moment, then stepped to the wash-basin and poured it down the drain. One after the other I drew the corks and poured the ale into the basin. As I emptied them I stood them up like soldiers on the floor.

I heard the boy's step on the back stairs. In he came cautiously. His rat-like, wicked little eyes peered around the room. He looked at the empty bottles on the floor—counted them—fifteen—chuckled—"My, but you're going a gait! And all alone, too!" And then, as if assured of something he very much wished to know, ran down the stairs again. I could hear the kitchen door closing behind him.

I threw the empty bottles out of the back window. I heard them drop one after the other, on the grass in the back yard. Then feeling drowsy, dull, tired—wretched—I undressed, and was getting into bed when Angus came in.

"A bad outlook for to-morrow, Ned." He had more beer, perhaps, than was really needful for his health, and so a bit maudlin. "The guv'nor give 'em the devil, Ned, and so did I—down to the Swan, Ned. But no use—twenty-five to one you can't win—and, of course, you can't—nor no man ever lived or ever will live, with that hound on the nine-yard mark. Well, well, I'll be turning in here to-night, Ned—spare beds enough." I must have gone off to sleep then, for I remembered no more of Angus.

The Christmas Handicap

But by and by, how much later I cannot say, I thought I heard a knocking at the door; at first softly, but at length more boldly. I sat up, and as I sat up it stopped, and as it stopped the voice of Angus called out: "What is it, Ned?"

"What's it, you?" I retorted; and must have immediately fallen off to sleep again, for I heard nothing more.

III

ONLY three bottles, and I knew men who could have taken a dozen of that same ale and not minded it, but the sap of life had long ago ceased to run freely in them, or else their natural holding caapcity was greater. I awoke like a man from horrid dreams, and had no appetite for breakfast, though I did try, under the anxious eye of Angus, to force it down.

"It can't be, Ned, you're stale from over-training. It can't be, for yesterday you were like a lion."

After breakfast I slipped down to the track, and had been cantering up and down for perhaps ten minutes, when Angus came running in. "What ails you, Ned—working like this on the morning of the finals?"

"I've got to work it off."

The Christmas Handicap

"Work what off?"

I made no answer to that, and he, thinking I
had a touch of the sulks, said no more; and I,
who had always laid out my own work, tore up and
down the track till I felt I had enough.

On the way back to the hotel I slipped Angus,
and, stepping into a pub, had a brandy and soda,
the second I had ever taken. The first was when
my wife had the baby, and I, in the next room,
had to wait hours for the word. As to drinking
that liquor, and drinking it when I did that morning in Sheffield, I have to say that I knew what I
was doing. There is more to training than exercising or being massaged, or eating or sleeping.
Ten years up to this time I had been running,
studying my game and studying myself. If I was
the fastest short-distance runner in the world, it
was more than length of stride or drive of back
and arm that made me so. It was more also than
my brains and body. It was knowing the things
which lie so deep in you that you are not able to
make anybody else understand them as you do
yourself. And that morning I drank my brandy
and soda, drinking it, too, in the full knowledge
that it is a bad thing, even one drink, when you
don't need it.

My drinking it was all over town in an hour,
and, joined to the rumor that I had been on a

drunk the night before, caused many a good man to grieve that day in Sheffield; and also it killed any further betting on me.

At half-past eleven o'clock I was back to the hotel. At twelve I had lunch—chops, soft-boiled eggs, toast, apple-butter, and tea. After lunch—one o'clock—I went to bed. The race was at four o'clock. "Call me at three," I told Angus—and was alseep, he said afterward, in two minutes.

At three o'clock I was sleeping so soundly that Angus had to shake me to wake me. At half-past three we went to the grounds, where were now forty thousand people, viewing patiently the preliminary events to keep them in humor; and they were still swarming in.

Not till I was on the mark that day did I get a look at Heddon. He *was* the man who only four months before I had run for the American hundred-yard championship. And now he had nine yards in a hundred and fifty. "Never, unless he drops dead, will you get him," was what one book-maker said to me, and that was pretty near what I thought myself.

"So it's you, you Australian champion," I said to Heddon when I met him. "A fine champion! And a fine game you're playing with Fifield."

"Well, it's so fine a game that when we cash in after the race we'll have back that four hundred pounds we lost in America and a good many other four hundreds with it."

"You have to win first."

He laughed out loud. "With nine yards? Ho, ho, with nine yards the devil from hell won't get me."

"Maybe the devil couldn't," I says—"but 'tisn't the devil will be after you. Poor devil, he has to hop along with cloven feet and a tail flying back in the wind to handicap him even more. But with *them* !" I held up one spiked shoe, and as he looked I flexed toes and instep, and—I couldn't help it, I was that alive with energy boiling to turn itself loose—I stood and leaped over a bench beside the track. It was a clean leap of eleven feet, toe to heel, and two fellows who had just finished a mile run were lying on it, resting. They started up in alarm. "Hi say, there, King—fancy if you didn't make it!"

"Make it!" broke in Angus. "Lie down. He could 'a' made it an you'd been tiered three high —and that's what he'll do to you, Heddon. Ned won't run this day—he'll leap the whole hundred and fifty yards. At about a hundred yards you want to listen—but you won't *have* to listen— you'll hear it—the chunk, chunk of his spikes, the same hitting the cinders so fast that you can't count 'em, and at a hundred and twenty you'll be

The Christmas Handicap

feelin' a hot breath getting hotter every second —and then you want to watch out, Heddon, for that 'll be the back-mark man comin' in to his own—won't it, Neddo?"

That sounded like blackguarding, didn't it? But this Heddon was a notorious man himself at that game, and we were only taking his measure; and not all foolishness, this by-play. As I watched him now I began to see that jump over the bench wasn't altogether a waste of energy. I knew what was running through his brain. He saw again that hundred and eighty odd pounds flying through the air. By and by that same hundred and eighty odd pounds would come flying through the air after him. When a lad and just breaking into the game, and faster men came tearing down behind me, I knew how I used to feel. I used to wish—with those champions behind me—I used to wish the tape was something nearer.

I was mad and getting madder. I could have ripped the track in two. I dug my holes, and, breaking away from the mark, breezed down past the stand. A voice there called out—an American voice, "There's your Derby winner for you— him for me."

I was beginning to feel like running, but I was not yet worked up to that nervous tension which precedes a great performance—or a great break-

The Christmas Handicap

down. Inside of me was—I began to feel it—the power with which, by and by, I would do what I willed. But as yet it half-slumbered.

Coming back by the judge's stand I met my old gaffer, whom I had not seen since the night before. All the morning I had been wondering where he had been. I thought he would say something about the brandy and soda; but evidently he had not yet heard of it. His face was beaming.

"You're a horse, lad—a horse, nothing less. But look here"—he stepped closer—"old Parkeson that couldn't be bribed—he's gone home for Christmas. Said in forty years he'd never failed to be home for Christmas eve—and they've bought up the substitute starter."

"Well, he'll need to be a clever one to shoot him off the mark and not me, too. When Heddon leaves the mark be sure I'll leave it with him—if I don't leave it before, so long as they're out to do that kind of work. But that fifty pounds the management's giving me for showing up—I want you to get it and lay it on me."

"To win? or for the place?"

"To win."

"Hah?" He laid a hand on my arm. "Have ye learned anything? Is aught wrong with 'im?"

"Nothing wrong with him. He'll run the race of his life to-day."

The Christmas Handicap

"Then ye can't win. At nine yards ye can't win. The devil from hell couldn't do it."

"That's what Heddon said, but I gave that devil's tail a twist, and he's not so sure as he was. At twenty-five to one, I'm telling you, lay that fifty pounds on me. Will you tend to it?"

"I will. And, by Heaven, a bit of my own. The fighting look's in your eye to-day, lad. And if you win—if you win, Ned——"

"If I win? What are you smiling at?"

"Ho, ho—it won't put me in the poor-house if we do lose. But keep an eye to the starter." He ran off toward the book-makers' stand.

"And get some of it with Fifield's people, if you can," I called after him.

"All they're game for," he called back.

The starter called out to know if I were ready. Always in the big handicaps it is the stratch-man who is deferred to. He it is who has the choice of paths, who may put off his preparations till the last second. In the light of the scratch-man's privileges I made my first move. One path was as good as another, but I wanted Heddon under my eye. He had the fourth path from the pole, so I demanded the third from the pole.

The starter seemed surprised. "I thought you'd already picked your path," and he pointed to where I had dug starting holes on the inside path.

"Ho, Ho, with nine yards the devil from hell won't get me"

The Christmas Handicap

"Never mind what *you think*," I rapped back. "It's what *I do* that you have to go by. I'm using my right to take what lane I please."

I took a long time digging my new holes, so long that all, Heddon and the starter particularly, began to show signs of nervousness.

When I had finished digging my holes I stood up in them, to get the feel of them in the usual way; after which I cast off my bath-robe. Angus, in waiting, picked it up and was about to make off down the track; but I looked at him, and he dropped it on the ground again. The others now handed their blankets to their attendants, who rushed off, as Angus would have done, down the track to where they would be able to see the finish.

We were now all ready—apparently. The starter said: "On your marks"—the others got on; so did I, but last of all and very slowly. "Get set," he called. All set—but me—and waited for the gun. I could, being behind, see them, but they could not see me. I made no move to set, but watched them for perhaps ten seconds. The starter, I knew, would never dare to fire that gun till I was ready at least—not with the eyes of sixty thousand people glued on us. He might be bought up, but 'twould be ruining him forever and taking his life in his hands to do that. Even at twenty-five to one, there was other money than our own down on me. Finally, he called out: "Come up, everybody—what's the matter, King?" at which I left my mark and jogged down the track.

I went fifty or sixty yards before turning back, and I made no haste coming back. The others, Heddon particularly, eyed me curiously. I paid no attention to them, except that, walking past Heddon, I said: "And you're dead sure you'll win it, eh?"

"What is it, King?" asked the starter.

"Oh—h—I don't know—nervous, maybe."

"Well, try it again." We set again. Again they bent quiveringly for the crack of the pistol, and again, at the instant when they were on the wrack to hear it, I stood up and, when the starter called "All up," swung down the track. This time I went a full hundred yards at almost top speed. Oh, but I was going rarely, and I made sure Heddon felt it. It was my day, and yet more than sheer sprinting power was to win this race for me.

Haskins, the pistol-firer, was plainly puzzled, and, I believe, worried by my actions, which was what I meant him to be. I had no mind to let him have that pistol-firing all to his own hand. He looked inquiringly at me as I returned to the mark, but I said nothing, only once more stood in my holes as if ready for the gun.

The Christmas Handicap

I watched again the backs and legs of my competitors as they crouched. They were all showing the strain. And yet again I stood up. This time I called out to Angus: "Just cinch up my shoe-lacings, will you, Angus?" and while he was bent over to it I, well wrapped in the bath-robe, whispered, "And take your time at it, Angus."

There I was warm as toast from my jogging and the bath-robe, and there they were beginning to feel the cold. Heddon darted down the track as I had been doing, but the others didn't dare to get too far off for fear the starter would make them hurry back and fire the gun before they had recovered their wind.

My shoes seemed laced to suit me, and, casting off the bath-robe, I was again on the mark. This time I meant to go.

I bent leisurely at the preliminary word, yet more leisurely at the word "Set"—taking notice of everybody, but with a special eye to Heddon. All by now were plainly showing the effect of being kept waiting. It was in December, Christmas eve, mind you, and, though a sunny day, naturally not over-warm, and men do not stay out in scant clothes, bare legs and arms and low-cut shirts without feeling it, and you want to be warm as a coal fire for your best sprinting. And more than the cool air they had been feeling the suspense of waiting. And Heddon? I knew how his mind was working. He was wondering if I would really go this time. "I'll worry you more than that," I said to myself, "with your nine yards and your crooked play. I'll worry you—and you, too,—Mister Starter."

I was going to try something I had never tried before in a race. They called me a steady and sure man on a mark—and so I was, none more so, but many a time had I tried this in practice. "As to the wrong of it," I argued to myself—"well, it may be, but they, not I, began the game." As to any wrong done to the other three in the race, they had no chance against Heddon or me. It was I or Heddon would win this race.

Well, there were sixty thousand crazy, howling people waiting for us to go, and a starter, for all he had fired the gun at a hundred handicaps, wishing to get the job off his hands. He said "Set," and there we were, I not quite steady, nor intending to be too quickly. But at last I bent over, and as I did so put my mind in place of the starter's. "Ah—h," he was saying to himself—"At last—and now—" and here he would be taking a quick, sure glance to the others and back to me again—"All steady now—" again a look all round—"A tremendous crowd—the biggest 'cap

The Christmas Handicap

in years—a good job almost done—and King still steady as a rock—and now——"

"Steady, Heddon! Steady, Heddon!" And Heddon already like a marble figure! That was the tip for him. "Now, Neddie boy, watch out," I said to myself.

Heddon's back hunched over so slightly, his knees moved. But he was not going just then. He relaxed—the others, mind you, like so many quivering rocks, as he no doubt thought I was, under the strain. I watched anew. The muscles of his back and legs began to crawl—a breath, and the heel of his front leg lifted, settled, the hind heel began to lift, l-i-f-t—a quick but full in-breath—and——

I leaped and the gun cracked. Nobody could say that I beat the gun or that Heddon beat the gun, but the starter had completed his contract. He had shot Heddon off his mark.

But Ned King was right there with him, not up into the air where a man a mile away could see, but moving out of the holes, nevertheless, and ten feet they say I cleared in that first wild leap from the mark.

"Blast you!" Angus later said I said, breaking out of the holes, but I don't remember that. I only remember that I saw Heddon before me, his back straight up, his head bobbing, his arms and legs working desperately. My back was bent over—no man running carried his body or head farther forward than I did; and my arms were swinging across my body, and hardly time to swing across before I had them back. My arms and back always did more of my running than my legs. Style? Style is made on a thousand practice days, not in the heat of the race. But I had style, none better, and I knew it was there to stand by me. And it was standing by me. Heddon ran high, with his legs moving like the fore legs of a trotting horse. Mine were more like the trotter's hind legs, my feet barely off the ground, but every stride well up on my toes, and a full eight feet to every stride at that after I settled down to my work. That was my job—to set my feet down and pick them up again as fast as ever I could. I hardly gave them time to hit the ground, though when they did hit it, they hit it for fair. They said afterward that a man who had to follow me down the track would have had his head knocked off with the cups of earth I threw behind. The track was a bit soft, I may say. They also said that you could hear me pounding a hundred yards away. Well, I meant to pound. I was after Heddon.

At thirty yards nobody could notice that I had gained. And maybe not. It took a few strides to get my weight and length under way; but after that nobody was heard to say that I did not gain; and gain fast. One chap with ten yards I caught at the hundred-yard post, though I only recall him dimly. I saw one man clearly in the race—Heddon—one man and one thing—Heddon and the red worsted across the track at the finish.

Heddon could run a fast hundred yards, and he ran a good hundred now. I gained no more than three yards on him, maybe four to the hundred-yard mark, which left all of five yards to make up in the last fifty. If a man can gain only four yards in a hundred, how can he ever gain nine in a hundred and fifty? It doesn't figure out, does it? No. But I could run every foot of a hundred and fifty yards. Heddon could not. Every yard that I covered saw me going faster than the yard before. He couldn't do that. He could run fast to a hundred, and there hold his speed. He could not increase it. Sprinting handicap rarely extends past a hundred and thirty-five yards, because they used to figure it out that a hundred and thirty-five yards is as far as the scratch-man can run without falling away in speed. But I knew that I could run a hundred and fifty and keep going faster and faster to the tape, on the right day, that is, and, believe me, this was the right day.

The Christmas Handicap

And I tore on with the same low stride and my body held forward like a rigid bar—every lift of my thigh beat against my ribs and chest. My breath was in-held, my heart pounding. And those others kept coming back to me, though, as I say, I barely saw them. But Heddon I saw. He loomed up immensely. The sixty thousand shrieking people—the insiders along the edge—I never saw or heard them. I never could see anybody in the race, anyway, but the man I had to beat. I don't know just where I passed the others, but I gave them a scandalous beating. At a hundred and twenty yards—thirty yards to go—only Heddon was before me—and he looked all over a winner. No mortal could beat a man of his speed four yards in thirty. But, God in Heaven, I was coming! Heddon's own backers were admitting that now. Never a man they ever saw was coming like me, they said. I, myself, did not believe then that I could win, but I still saw Heddon's back. He was still going, and going good, but, God in Heaven, I was tearing, leaping—flying, man, flying.

Ten yards from the finish and the Heddon people cheered crazily for their victory. It was as surely all over as that. And I heard that cheer. Through my ears, and into my brain, yes. I could'nt hear sixty thousand people, but I could feel the taunt in that yell, and into my soul it came —and then—then I lifted. Hope of Heaven, man, but I lifted. Back, arms, shoulders, neck, the muscles of my toes, the very scalp on my head —I gave 'em all I had. Man, but 'twas a burst.

They said I covered twenty-five feet in my last two strides. In the last foot of that last leap I got him.

That's the way I stormed at the finish; and past the line I kept on going, arms down, head up again, but my momentum carrying me clear on to the turn of the track fifty yards beyond the finish, and there at the curve I almost ran over the fence and into the people in the front row of seats, who by this time were making a run for the field; and it was there I almost ran into her arms—and her arms were wide open. She crying—calling, "Oh, Eddie—Eddie—"and the little one laughing like mad, "Oh, papa—papa—" she was saying, and, believe me, I didn't regret that finish.

Thousands of voices were calling—some yelling—some cheering—cursing, some of them—but when I heard her voice, and the name—she alone ever called me "Eddie"—I clean forgot Fifield and the beautiful beating I intended giving him the minute after the race was over. It was almost smothered, that voice, and I was excited, confused—even now it blurs to me—but I whirled, and stood on my toes. Being tall, I soon saw her —little as she was—herself and the little one. I shoved them right and left when they wouldn't make way, and little I cared what they might think, I lifted her off her feet and kissed her, and snuggled her—and hoisted the little girl to my shoulder.

About this time the gaffer came running down with his watch in his hand: "D' y' know what ye did, Ned—do ye know, man?"

"I don't know, and I don't care," I said.

"Man, man, but the most impossible time— an impossible time." He repeated it reverentially.

I went to the dressing-room, leaving my wife and child to go to their hotel with my gaffer. After dressing I sneaked out of the grounds through a loose plank in the fence—to dodge the crowd— and by side streets stole up to my own hotel to get my bag. I was coming down the stairs again when I met the bar-maid. She was taking off her hat. She looked at me and I looked at her. I shook hands with her and said: "I'm going."

"I know. I saw the race—and the rest of it." There was that in her expression that made my heart bleed, but what could I do?

Out on the street I recollected the note of the night before. When I had put it in my pocket I meant to read it later. Now I drew it out and

I could feel the taunt in that yell, and into my soul it came

tore it into little pieces which I scattered along the gutter. I had no mind now to read it.

At the other hotel, the best in the city, in our suite of rooms, we had dinner. The old gaffer had collected all the money due us, and that money was now poured into a great salad-bowl. In five and ten pound notes and sovereigns it flowed over the edges of the bowl, for us to look at while we ate.

I poured my share, more money than I expected to earn in years, into my wife's lap. "There's your little house in the country and something more. Forgive me those two thousand dollars I gambled away. Forgive me for leaving you as I did."

The tears stood in her eyes.

"And forgive *me*, Ned," put in the gaffer. "I do love a game man, and you're game. When you told me your story, after you'd won that second 'cap, I couldn't help writing her. And I knew more of Fifield than I ever let on. I've a friend or two in America, too. But I was afraid for the missus—afraid she'd get here too soon and interfere with your trainin'. And afraid she'd come too late and make no Christmas for you. And now that's said, there's for the kiddie." He crowded ten gold sovereigns in each of the child's hands. Money looked so common to us that when the sovereigns rolled out of her little hands, we none of us bothered to help her collect them, but let her chase them around the floor, under the table and chairs.

And that night I made up my mind never to run again. That day I had beat the gun—the only crooked thing I ever did.

That side of it didn't bother my gaffer.

"Don't let that worry you—'twas you or them, with them naming the rules. But if you never run again, Ned, here's this from me." He stood up to say it. "I've seen 'em all, Ned, in the last fifty years—seen 'em all come and go—but you're the greatest of 'em all. And I'm not in wine when I say it—Ned, you're the greatest sprinter that ever laced a shoe."

'Twas worth putting your soul to the wrack to be told that by him, the best judge of sprinters and the best-hearted old gaffer in England.

That night, for the first time in most four months, I felt a woman's arm about me. And next day was Christmas.

216 7230